THERE'S ALWAYS A GIRL

stories short & long

Barry Spacks

For One & Only
Kimberley

With thanks to the editors of the journals in which
several of these stories first appeared in earlier forms:
THE QUARTERLY REVIEW OF LITERATURE
THE CARLETON MISCELLANY
VAGABONDAGE PRESS

painting on front cover, "One-Frame Movie" by Barry Spacks
portrait of Barry Spacks on back cover by Jack Smith
photo of Hedy Lamarr from Tradebit, Inc.

typesetting: Diane Collins
cover: Kachergis Book Design

CONTENTS

THE BEARD

*Only put off until tomorrow what you are willing
to die having left undone.*

— *Picasso*

"THIS HARVARD BOY YOU'D REPLACE," said Uncle
Tommy, "I don't hear from him oh, four, five weeks, it turns out
he's in court, it's probation, Harvard gives him the boot, drugs,
he's involved with some kind of weird Chinese business." Uncle
shrugged. "But that's an exception, mostly these boys they work
for me around the country, they're young married men like you,
Robert, it's a help to them to get through school. Believe me, my
boys from way back, they send pictures, letters...."

Uncle Tommy. Does even God know his real name? Two
years married, I was looking for summer work through the B.U.
Placement Service, wound up with an interview and as soon as he
saw my beard Uncle Tommy offered me the job.

He designed and manufactured kiddies' banks, cheap toys
really, to be sold or given away as premiums by real banks. "I was
first in the business," he informed me. "Later come along a lot of
schleppers, my competition, but where's one with ethical standards
or a bright idea? When I make a bank it holds up, a child can
mess with it, it won't fall apart in your hands."

He displayed some of his earlier models, a tiny gumball machine
and a red plastic cash register, an edible one in the shape of an
elephant made out of flavored wax ("a dumb item, I'm ashamed
of it") a dog that wagged its tail, a monkey that tipped its hat, and

1

a bank from the previous Christmas that danced, a typical Uncle bank, wildly-retro, I'll have to describe it to demonstrate what sort of set-up I was getting myself into.

Made of tin, painted tin, about four inches high, with a key wind-up that caused two teenagers on a red base to jounce about. It was called "The Thrift," they were dancing *the thrift*, until the boy-doll in his black motorcycle jacket tilted forward with the dime in his mouth that triggered the device and neatly shot the sidewise dime into the wide, expectant mouth (a deep money-kiss) of the girl-doll, after which the little couple fell apart, becoming as still as two switched-off seven-watt bulbs (there's symbolism wherever you look for it).

When the girl-doll and the base were chock full of dimes, the kid or the parents were supposed to take the money out — she split right down the middle — take the coins and start an actual savings account at a real bank for the kid who'd been wheedling dimes from family friends and relatives in the first place. *Thrift* was the idea, the training of young people in the virtue of thrift, patience and so on, and most of these banks were sold for the Christmas season, so Uncle's part-time salesmen did the rounds mainly in the summer and early fall.

"The Thrift" made a sound throughout the savings-operation best represented as *beep-beep*. There was something funny and pathetic about the sounds these banks made. But you couldn't laugh at Uncle Tommy, not unless he started it first by joking about his own enthusiasm, because kid banks were his life's work, produced at a small factory outside Chicago with Tommy himself going all over the country hiring salesmen and slipping them emergency supplies right out of the scaled-down box of a semi-trailer he drove, where he sometimes even slept, it turned out, on a cot in there among the bank cartons. This was before electronics made his whole business entirely obsolete.

So he took me out to demonstrate the sales approach. We went in a cab, his truck laid up at the time in a garage in Framingham.

My beard had gotten him excited. I'd been wearing this beard for about a year, partly because I'd begun balding while still an undergraduate, partly because I'd always found it a drag to shave, and undoubtedly for a hundred obscure reasons, sane or silly or depth-psychological, because in an old photo I encountered my father with a beard, a little Hungarian chinbrush (whereas mine at full flower formed a bushy semi-circle) — because I was thirty one and dying of graduate school and a wife and baby and a dinky shack of an apartment miles from campus and no confidence in my so-called talent and wasting away my life.

Death by marriage.

In any case I had a beard, and that immediately got me the summer job, because the new bank Tommy wanted to sell, this new bank also had a beard, one with a canny resemblance to my own. I had to laugh when I saw myself as a bank, but this was a laugh as if from someone who'd just been operated on for a hernia.

"Sonny," said Uncle Tom, "please don't be sensitive about your whiskers, you're going to make a fortune out of this, believe me, it's like the Planter's Peanut Man dressed up like a peanut!"

"That's me," I said. The word *Beatnik* still retained a certain currency then, used as a vague insult for outsider types, so Uncle's latest tinny invention was called *The Banknik*. It had my beard (black-dyed rabbit fur), my red-rimmed eyes, my weary rabbinical air. You pushed a coin into its mouth, the eyes opened up, the lips yielded a rubbery smile, and a sound occurred as the coin clinked down within, a sound like a single peep out of a starving baby bird.

I should mention that I was involved then in earning a Ph.D. in art history at B.U., that I hadn't really worked hard at paintings of my own for what felt like years, that there was always a major money problem in our household, and that my wife Muriel had become rapidly ennobled through suffering mainly brought about by my own dissatisfactions and despairs — this was our situation in capsule version — and there I was sitting beside Uncle Tommy in the cab, moving along the wide sweep of river across from M.I.T., dozens of sails on the water, some blue, some white, veering and tacking out in the sweet sunshine, kids walking, summer school students strolling or reading or making out on the grass, scullers sculling, everything blooming. Tom took me off to South Boston somewhere to learn how you sell bankers a bearded kid-bank with a resemblance to the salesman's own hungry face.

"You know what I tell my boys, my salesmen?" said Uncle Tom as we turned onto the Expressway. "I tell them a kid is better off saving dimes, getting used to the American way, otherwise he's buying airplane glue to sniff or worse, so I say they should be proud, they're a real part of the war on moral decadency."

"Only you're not going to lay all of that on me, are you, Uncle Tom? The War On Moral Decadency?"

"No," he wheezed, beginning to laugh, "I won't, I won't say it, because" — I thought he would choke — "that's a load 'a crap." His cough continued and after a while I started pounding him on the back. "Thank you," he said, wiping his eyes. He pointed to a bragging sign painted large on the wall of a furniture discount house we were passing: TWENTY THREE YEARS AND NEVER A SALE. "They're proud of it?" he joked, "with business that bad?"

He was a sweet, comical old guy at heart, his blue eyes self-mocking and sad. There was a touch of old-world coziness about him, you could picture him shambling around in carpet slippers in a house full of rocking chairs, wearing one of those cardigans with leather-knot buttons.

Okay. On the steps of this bank where I'd get my salesman's initiation — we'd come all this way because Tom knew one of the vice-presidents — he stopped for a little lecture. "Now rule one I want you to remember, Robert, please, you call a man by his first name. Always a friend to friend basis, get it? Just watch how I sell, you'll see. Rule two, and listen, when you know you got a

4

disinterested party, go yourself and open a little savings account, it costs what, a few bucks, and there's the deposit book in your hand, so you walk in on him again and you're a customer already. Come, I'll show you. You should see my income tax with interest from a million little *pishka* savings accounts I got to write down."

We entered this bank on Congress Avenue somewhere through an Ionic portico into a hall so large it was like South Station, locomotives could have chugged back and forth in there. A century ago this bank might have serviced crowds, but now there were no customers to speak of, they'd gone on to banks that looked like high-class motels. Here the tellers stood in little cages counting money while behind a wooden railing sat minor officials looking glum, no opportunities for advancement, no inspirations forthcoming for schemes of embezzlement, just bored to tears.

It turned out that Tommy's vice president wasn't with them anymore. We were directed to an office in the rear where they had a honeycomb of partitions, and feeling like the sacrifice at the end of a short procession, I trudged along behind Uncle Tommy.

Beyond the little labyrinth of partitions we entered the office of somebody in advertising and public relations, a large bald man in a linen suit, I can't recall his name. Tommy beamed at him like a light on the sea. The man said he was very busy but Tommy offered to buy five minutes of his time. "No," Tom said, "believe me, why shouldn't I pay for your valuable attention?" But then he shifted away from that offer somehow, displaying the *Banknik,* calling attention to my beard, telling this large advertising man that in the small town of West Wroncher, PA, population oh maybe eight, ten thousand, well, his salesman happened to take a survey among the gang-member boys and listen, talk about getting those kids back on the savings-path...it becomes painful to continue in detail at this point. Poor Tommy, he just sold and sold, pitched and pitched, he was still selling and pitching as the ad-man eased us out of there, still talking about gang-intervention via little savings banks as we retreated through the church-like

5

hush of the main chamber, the tellers still busy counting their money, the minor officials still glum and woebegone.

I noticed that Tommy was breathing rather heavily. "Don't let that shake your enthusiasm," he said out on the portico. "It happens. It happens. You run into a guy with no love for children." He laughed, coughed. "I could take it over his head, get to know the bank president on a first-name basis, but that for me is a last resort."

"You're going to go at him again?"

"No, Robert. You. You're going to pester it right out of him. Say in a month's time."

"Me? Don't you think he's had enough already?"

"Listen," said Uncle Tommy, "is that a way to talk if you want to make a sale? You're the *Banknik-man*, Robert. You're in business, you got to start taking life, you know, seriously."

By the time I arrived home at the apartment in the late afternoon, carrying a carton of a dozen sample *Bankniks* and my order blanks and such, I felt entirely remote from the man I'd been — painter, teacher, husband, father — when I'd set out to meet Uncle Tommy earlier that day. Now I was the *Banknik-man*.

"Where were you so long?" said Muriel. "Did they offer you the job?"

"I survived," I told her. "See? Intact. Still sound of limb." I sat down, exhausted. "Why do you always look like you're about to get bad news every minute?"

"Well, you were gone so long I was worried."

Today, remembering the tremor in her speaking voice, a feeling of tenderness, a sort of wave of sweetness takes me over, lifts me gently and eases me down. But at the time I had no patience with her, I had it worked out that she was the real source of my lousy incapacities and compromises and anxieties. She asked if I'd go down the street to the store to get the baby some strained bananas. At that moment I knew what bank robbers and blackmailers and so on want to say to the police when they're caught;

6

they want to say, "I have a wife, a baby, we had to get married... what else could I do?"

The baby began to cry. I went to the door. "Go back to your mother-work, Busty," I told Muriel. "Nurse the poor bastard, give him strength so when I drop out he can grow a beard to pay the rent on this crummy hole."

The funny thing was, I really started selling the damned *Bankniks*, once my stomach grew strong enough to let me trade on the beard and the recommended whimsy. Uncle Tom's approach, the survey of West Wroncher Hoodniks, went over for me like a load of sand. The bankers I ran into, the purchasing agents and advertising vice-presidents, when it came to children they seemed to figure that you were supposed to feed them and spank them and that should suffice. I would have just been ushered right back out into the carbon monoxide if I'd stuck to Tommy's save-the-youth spiel, because it was hot, everybody I tried to sell was in danger of falling asleep, my old car moved in traffic like swimming through a pot of thick vegetable soup. All appeals to patriotism, capitalism, community service, pride, gluttony, lust, failed to work. So I started clowning. I went in not giving a damn, popped a coin in my mouth, rolled my eyes, smiled at them, making like a *Banknik*, and the bankers chuckled a little and signed the order blanks and I walked back out a slightly richer man, able to buy my son his little Gerber bottles of strained bananas. He was hooked on those strained bananas, I'll tell you.

It was July, what I really wanted was to return to the apartment and have a nice pornographic dream, but I kept driving from stop to stop on my list, hitting about seven banks on a really good afternoon. (It's unbelievable how many banks there are in a single urban area — have a look in the phone book). I amused myself between stops by working out plans for a hold-up of the last place I'd been, like through the sewers and the drainpipes ("Cripes, the Sewer Rat, he's knocking off the First Federal through the drainpipes, this is a job for the Green Hornet, or better yet, for *Submariner!*"). Most of the small branch banks could have been robbed simply by cutting the cord to the air-conditioning: everybody inside would have fallen immediately into a sweaty siesta.

It wasn't only the joke of the beard and my clowning that fetched them. About the second week I happened on a device that I suppose is a commonplace to professional commission salesmen, but it came to me with the power of revelation. This was to offer to bet my commission that the kid banks would sell, or be given away to new accounts, that such-and-such a number would go before the end of the year if they'd just set them up beside the tellers' cages like I told them, with the little posters. The bet was a joke, like me popping a silver dollar in my mouth and making 'em crack up in the aisles (*You card! You singin' fool!*). But one guy actually wanted to bet instead of being charmed by my bearded intensity. This was a man into whose office I'd been led while he was reading a racing sheet, which, with a banker, is like catching the matron of a girl's finishing school orgying with the board of trustees.

"I have a proposition," I told one guy when he'd expressed disinterest and failed to applaud my silver dollar stunt. "Will you listen to a proposition?"

"We hardly know each other," this guy said.

Oh, bankers are comics too, believe me. We're all people here. I told the gambling banker with his racing sheet that I'd bet my commission he'd move them all by Christmas if he ordered, say, two gross of *Bankniks*. "Gross," he said, "appropriate word." But he did order, and we did bet, and he actually paid off: I got a check for exactly ten bucks in the mail the following May.

I learned something from all of this: that business, the kiddy-bank business, anyhow, was a cinch, you only needed a gimmick, and if that didn't work, you needed a different gimmick, and eventually you'd be a millionaire and your son could spit his strained bananas in your face when he came home on vacation from NYU with his roommate who would be, naturally, the head of the college anarchists. The more commission I made, the worse it became. I was suffering that summer and early fall from a sense of being a successful member of the middle class, tiny checks arriving from Uncle Tom from all over the country, along with his post cards full of exclamation points and little verbal shrugs: "A boy from Colorado College I didn't hear from him, it turns out he commits suicide on me!"

Tommy rolled through town again in October, by which time I'd about covered my area. My son was fat on strained bananas, Muriel seemed noticeably less anxious and I was assisting in an undergraduate studio lab and painting mud on canvas and pacing around like a tenor with lockjaw and going out three afternoons a week selling *Bankniks*, selling them, with my routine down so sweet I only had to walk through the door and the bankers started laughing and flailing around with their fountain pens. "What do you mean you can't sell these things?" I'd say. "Put them in a little pyramid in the lobby and immediately in comes a troop of boy scouts, they're touring the civic facilities, believe me, I've got them waiting around the corner right now in mark-step, as soon as you sign, you'll see, in they come with their money in their mouths."

"What did I tell you?" said Uncle Tommy, elated, relaxing in the imitation Danish armchair Muriel had bought with the help of the last checks from him to come through. "Did I tell you there was a talent here, or not? What do you think of this boy, Mrs. Levi, eh? Isn't he something?"

My wife, in her usual state of hysteria when she had to prepare supper for more than one, called in from the kitchen that I sure was something, all right. "He's doing better than my others," Uncle Tommy called to her. "His first year. I'm so proud of him I could bust!"

Muriel came in carrying a pan of sizzling chicken and said she was proud of me too and gave us both a deranged smile and disappeared again to continue the sound of deep-fat frying. The baby crawled all over Uncle Tommy. We ate. I poured out cheap red wine. Uncle told us about his travels, his customized semi-trailer parked illegally out front, kids writing expressive statements on its dusty sides. Into the calm as we lapped up our store-bought chocolate pudding I told Uncle that it looked like I was finished with the *Banknik* business.

"What are you talking?" He seemed astonished. "I plan to keep this particular bank on right through next year, Robert. You covered the local outlets, so now it's time to spread yourself a little, wait, I've got good news to tell you, soon as we finish with this lovely meal." He made a fine, hat-tipping gesture to Busty in the absence of a hat, "which, believe me, I haven't had home-cooked like this in a month of Sundays. I got some big ideas for you, super-salesman!"

"No," I told him, "I'm through. Believe me." Muriel gave me her worried look, refilling the coffee cups. "I can't concentrate on my painting, I've got to settle in and get some real work done."

"Real work? What real work? Listen, you're a genius, you're the *Banknik* man, what are you talking?"

"He's awfully good, isn't he?" said Busty, "We've both been just amazed. He's a natural salesman."

"Of course," said Uncle, "of course, what else? Now listen, children, consider the possibilities. First I thought I'd offer more territory, the suburbs, etcetera, but it don't make sense. I mean, I could eventually give Robert the whole of New England, but where would that put us? So let me tell you my idea."

He proceeded to sketch it out, drawing charts with his fingernail on the tablecloth. I was to be his promotion manager. I'd fly to the West Coast, for example, interview the college boys out there, show them how the firm wanted their beards to look. I'd train them, I'd teach them how to fake-swallow silver dollars without choking, how to roll their eyes like the *Banknik*, and how to slap the bankers on the back and set up displays at conventions and eventually, in addition to salary and commissions and

10

expenses, there'd be a little share of the business for me...who else would Uncle look out for if not his Robert, practically his partner in the firm already, and in my spare time I could still paint if I wanted to, and study art and teach and like that.

What got me was how Muriel took it all in with perfect respect, and I was ready to explode from the way she listened to him, about to send fragments of my balding skull and tufts of my stupid beard to splatter all over the forsythia pattern on the wallpaper.

"A man should work where his talent is," said Uncle Tommy.

"What do you think?" said Muriel, my good, well-meaning, big-breasted helpmate, my rib, my clumsy cross, my vinegar and myrrh.

"Look," said Uncle Tommy, "you'll make fun of me, Robert, but even for fun I brought along your certificate like I give the boys. I had it framed."

He took from his briefcase a document in a Woolworth's frame which I actually kept hanging for years. It announced impressively that I had done my stint of public service keeping at-risk children off the streets, teaching them "through the sale and promotion of entertaining banking devices," the virtue of thrift upon which a nation's greatness depends.

"Very funny," I told him. "I'll treasure this."

"How come you're so sad, Robert?" He leaned forward from the egg-shaped Danish chair, purchased at a discount from Muriel's furniture-dealer cousin. The baby had begun to cry and she'd gone off to deal with him. I said: "You're really very kind, Uncle Tom. I mean, it's nice of you..."

"Nice? Believe me, this proposition, it's not nice, it's smart." And then he surprised me, he said: "Don't be a snob, Robert."

"How do you mean?"

"You shouldn't act like your work is beneath you, understand? Nothing good comes from feeling like that. Your wife can tell you, you should trust her reactions. Listen, forgive me, what kind

of future do you have with this painting business? You understand me, Robert? You're the kind of boy people like to give him
a hand. It's a gift, and some have it and some don't, that's all."

"And the people who have it, they're all set up to be great
salesmen?"

"Salesmen, sales managers, nobody can do enough for them.
A man with a gift like that, he makes a person feel good in his
feelings, so he'll break his neck for him, he'll buy, he'll sell...listen,
Robert, I'm not just talking to a college boy, a graduate student
here, it's like my own son I'm talking to..."

"Maybe I'll sell my paintings then eventually, Uncle Tommy?
If I have the gift like you say?"

"Sure," he murmured, his expression hard. "If it's a question of
selling, why not?" And then: "That's why you paint your pictures?
To sell them?"

I told him I'd let him know about his offer. I said I'd think it
over and drop him a line. But he knew, all right, and when he left
he seemed depressed, shaking his head as he went down the walk
to his custom-semi. I watched him struggle up into the cab. The
truck roared and slowly eased from the curb. I took up my certificate, stared at my name written in there among the resounding
phrases.

My certificate.

I went to the bathroom then, and with my paper scissors and
my father's old Rolls razor, I took off the beard.

In the mirror my face looked like an animal startled in the
depth of night by a flashlight pointed into its burrow. My face
had a defenseless look and I felt very tender and protective toward
it.

I came into the bedroom where Muriel was tilted up in bed,
reading. She gave a start, seeing my face, and a little moaning cry.
"Oh, baby," she said, "why did you do that?"

I stretched out beside her, rubbed my smooth chin along the
top of her head, along her cheek. I held her. I rubbed away her

tears with my strange new face. The way our faces met, it was like two lovers coming together without any clothes on.

I wanted her to pose for me. Holding the baby. I already had a gesso'd canvas ready, untouched for months in the back room. In the morning, when she was free, maybe we'd get started. I joked to myself that it could be a monumental work. People would stand in awe before it right through the ages.

"Tell me," I said. "Tell me I'll make it as a painter."

"Of course you will, Baby. No question. It's all gonna turn out fine."

"You think so? Be honest."

"Come here. Come to Momma. Yes. That's good. Of course you'll make it. Believe me. I'm going to insist on that. You're my genius husband. You're a beautiful painter, Robert. You really are!"

THE HE AND THE SHE OF IT

Every telling has a tailing and that's the he and the she of it.

— *Joyce, Finnegans Wake*

SEVERAL TIMES I PLAYED ROUGH with Andrew, but this was the worst.

"Remove that robe," I ordered, clenching my eyes.

"I'm to remove my robe?'

"You got it, Buster." Movie-level talk takes over in a crisis.

"Exactly what did you have in mind?"

At those words, Gloria let out a snort of laughter, struggling to shrug on her peasant skirt while I wrestled the ridiculous robe from Andrew's concave-chested, ribby body. Below he wore only blue briefs. The style's now called "Speedo." Within Andrew's Speedo came a certain bulging. "Off with the shorts," I commanded. I wasn't about to make this happen with my own hands. "Do it, Andrew!" I bulked up at my most threatening. I've sometimes been compared, in my hairiness and menace, to a bear, and, truth is, I wasn't much of an admirable guy back then, not the sort of person I'd enjoy running into today. We're involved here, Reader, with a shameless confession masquerading as a piece of fiction.

Andrew let down his blue shorts and everything turned blue. Released from the constraint of the garment, perhaps stimulated by my threatening ways, who knows, a veritable Andy of a projectile lofted as with the sound of a sprong. The display was impressive — not exactly what I'd intended. Gloria laughed, clasping her

15

bra behind, and for a moment I almost credited their improbable claim that she'd only agreed to model for him in his room. But even that much intimacy threatened to unnerve me. Movie-words again, but how else describe a pain to your being as if you were suddenly churned to the state of an inner soup by a stone-crunching-machine? I'd found my girl naked in another guy's room and instantly was reduced to a surge of primitive emotion.

I haven't told Gloria to this day, now that we're back in contact a bit by e-mail, how much the sheer excitement of her madness had meant to me at the time. I hated the thought that any part of her might have been shared, even with a nice, talented guy like Andrew, and — let's say — only visually. In my self-important twenty-seventh year, there in Andrew's room in the graduate dorms, a brute impulse took me over.

"I warn you I'm feeling kind of outraged, Andy."

"Elton, keep calm," Gloria whispered. "Nothing happened!" Meanwhile Andrew's hands tried comically to fig-leaf his unsheathed groin.

"Just thought we should have a little viewing of the golden boy," I told her. "What were you thinking, Gloria? Jesus! That I'd assault your lad? Ruin your evening?"

"May I put my robe back on? It's chilly..."

"...shut up. Lie down on the bed."

He did. One-masted.

What next?

Well, what more? I controlled myself. "Enjoy your little experiment," I spat, and got out of there. But not before I'd impulsively grabbed from his desk a sheaf of Andy-papers that proved, on inspection, to consist of many of his early poems. Those priceless, handwritten manuscript pages — with their substantial influence on my own developing style — he never saw again.

16

2.

To make sense of the situation in Andrew's room I have to go back to the so-called "office" of our campus poetry journal earlier that day, a publication with a minute circulation noted locally for its experimental attitude since its birth during the G.I. university influx after the Korean War. It was in this room a few weeks earlier that I'd first met the guy I call Andrew in these pages, an ambitious Brit graduate student on some kind of fellowship that situated him with the rest of us in our eastward-leaning sector of the Midwest.

We're talking here of a time way back in the late American 50's, or as Andrew would quip, "during the French and Indian Wars." At a mere twenty-three he'd already become quite an inventive writer, though naturally not as yet well-known. He'd tripoded into a lit First at Cambridge the year before (Pembroke College, home of Milton and Spenser) and, once settled in the graduate dorms that September and teaching Freshman comp like the rest of us, he'd volunteered for editorial work on the magazine *Sheaves* — a boyish guy, attractive despite his British badness of teeth; tall, sunny, body frail in an appealing sort of way. He frequently flashed an engaging smile, jaggedness of questionable teeth notwithstanding, and seemed to sport a substantial appetite for the sensuous and sensual for a polite Brit of his generation. Take a look at him devouring a ripe Georgia peach, note the juices flowing down his chin, and you'll see what I mean.

This Andrew, randomly encountered, turned out to color my imaginative experience in various ways for the rest of my life. He offered the lean and hungry Brit look popular in the States back then, floppy auburn hair, narrow face, touchingly narrow shoulders.

And if you suspect, given Andrew's fake name and our obscured location, that I'm inventing at random, I answer *No more than God does*. It's just that A.N. grew eventually so grand — even

17

winding up as *Sir* Andrew, believe it — that trouble from his family could result if these recountings ever managed to fall into the public sphere, plus I'd gone and borrowed for keeps those valuable manuscript copies I'd mentioned of his early poems. So — even in a private and otherwise unshielded account — this out-of-the-mainstream British poet will appear in nominal drag as *Andrew Norton*. And me? I'm literary enough to say *Don't call me Ishmael*. Fuck it, no disguises — I'm the poet and professor Elton Gold.

3.

The tiny magazine *Sheaves* emerged from an appropriately tiny space containing one desk, three vintage slat-back wooden seats lined against the wall as if for naughty students, and a leatheresque desk chair on casters paired to another desk across a short, narrow corridor declared to be a room. Please note as well two tall, chipped yellowish-green metal bookcases flanking the smaller desk, these stocked with papers, files, multi-copies of previous issues of the magazine, plus books ready to be eviscerated, realigned, explained, or maligned via the then near-universal cult of *New Criticism*.

At that afternoon's meeting, Gregory Mamoolian, editor of *Sheaves*, addressed the magazine's complete editorial board, namely Andrew, Gloria Zizzic, and me.

"Gents and lady," Mamoolian declared, a large, smiling, affable English Department lecturer somewhere in his thirties, dressed in signature grey Athletic Department sweatshirt with hood, voluminous brown drawstring trousers, sandals with white socks. "Cohorts," he teased, "mighty decisions lie before us, aesthetic calculations that may well alter the course of nations. Shall we move briskly along and vote on our final choices for the next issue of *Sheaves*?"

Andrew had been in the country and on campus for less than a month at the time, his Ph.D. project a study of various 20th century literary figures among the Midwestern colonials, emphasis on Sinclair Lewis. "Cohorts," he offered, exactly mimicking Mamoolian's louche tone and vocabulary, "I've read and re-read these so-called poems in the final cut, and they do seem — how shall I put it? — woefully drab."

Gloria and I chuckled at "woefully drab," then called out in unison "Hear-hear, Andrew!" Years later we might have followed with high-fives. Mamoolian for his part feigned chagrin, yet couldn't resist adding a bark of approving laughter.

"Let's devote the whole issue to Andrew's stuff," Gloria suggested with surprising solemnity. More about her later. At this point she simply added: "The Complete Works of Andrew Norton! Think about it. And I could do some little line-drawings to break things up, like in *The New Yorker*."

I must pause to explain that when Andrew first joined the staff we all three had a listen at his sheaf of poems, twenty pages or so that he read aloud. When he'd finished, in that same office, Gloria's immediate response was a surprised "whoa!" This was not the sort of work we could have anticipated, given Andrew's gentle voice and shy good manners. Every poem in the batch served as an experiment, darting in from a curious angle, some rather erotically raw from a Brit visiting in the Midwest in 1957. I can't deny that as a poet I've learned one hellova lot myself from "Andrew Norton."

Here's a tiny taste, typically untitled, drawn from my stolen stash of Norton juvenilia:

> *narrow the gap between hush & silence*
> *the ocean creaks like an idiot captain:*
> *taste the salt*

Yes, that's all of it. Read it again if you like. I'll wait.

See?

"Whoa," was my comment, echoing Gloria's, "what have we here?"

4.

I've been for untellable years what's called "a poet in the academy," a man obligated by tradition to shock and dismay his ivy-covered colleagues. Back in '57, however, I was just another hopeful grad student and teaching assistant like Gloria and Andrew, busy researching my dissertation on Eudora Welty, a relatively obscure figure at the time. I'd survived Korea as an enlisted man, rising to the rank of Corporal, imagine, having joined after graduation from the U. of C. specifically in order to avoid a proffered graduate school fellowship with attached deferment. Sure enough, immediately after my army tour — which saw the U.S. through to the détente at the DMZ — I decided to partake of the G.I. Bill to cool out with a little post-carnage graduate education, choosing this quiet campus and never looking back, sweating to publish up the ranks, moving on from U. to U. "in residence."

But we were discussing Andrew. The two of us had some hard times. Yet why finger over old wounds at so late a date? Why kvetch and caper in memory of ancient pains and hi-jinx? Ah, as they say, *it's what we do.* Life goes unceasingly along with its stories and we try to get at least some parts right. There's a little Andrew-like two-line poem of my own that touches on this question of aspiration:

> *We've been here all along, yet still*
> *Keep hoping to arrive.*

5.

I'd been besotted with Gloria Zissic since the autumn before, but lo, anyone could see she already felt libidinally drawn toward A.N.'s Nottingham accent as smoothened by his Cantab years. She literally veered toward the boy physically there between us against the wall in the Sheaves office. Gloria liked to say her ambition was to be Emma Bovary without the arsenic. She projected a force — perverse, maddening, opinionated — by which I couldn't fail to be mesmerized. I'd yearned from childhood to avoid the fate of an overfed timidity, so rebels like Gloria, dead set against convention, couldn't help but leave me enthralled. Did I love her? Isn't obsession just as good? I held to her with an attitude of heart-crushing awe. I've always treasured the risk of being with a Crazy Girl.

At the office she'd sat there smiling like a carriage'd queen after suggesting the all-Andrew issue.

"Radical idea," said Editor Mamoolian. "But won't we come up with a lot of complaints from submitters passed over?"

Andrew, a bit pop-eyed and seemingly in shock, remained silent. Then: "I'm touched. Cohorts! That you would even consider such an honor! But I'd best stay out of these deliberations."

"Fair enough" commented Mamoolian, his omnipresent briar burbling away.

It seemed my turn, as a brother-poet, to further green-light the notion, and indeed my more generous side rose up. "Let's go for it," I concurred, "it's something different for poor old *Sheaves*, plus a nice splashy way to welcome Andy to the Great Republic of American Letters."

I learned from the adoring glance A.N. cast my way that this might have been the first time he'd been called *Andy* in public. Welcome to America.

An entire issue of *Sheaves*, stocked with Andrews' stuff. Well, we did it. With line-drawings by Gloria the Zizzic. "Something different," yes — prophetic words. My temptation is to incorporate at this point a little sample of what A.N. was up to poetically as of that stage in his career, so wildly influenced as he was by experimental writing on our side of the pond. But best to avoid major detours while traveling the roadways of a story — I'll record just one Andrew piece, a favorite of mine among the items in the all-Andy issue.

DILEMMA OF THE FAT CATS

The bamboo leaves attempt a take-off
    at every flighty whim of the wind
but the stalks try their best not to let them go.

This should be seen as an emblem for fat cats
    who grow so tragic-attached to themselves
they can never reach our enlightened South,

which explains why their rage seeks to sweep them away
    the opposite way, past law's Great Wall
where the chance plot-points of a network opus

stirs them to reach for a lethal ice-dagger,
    a jury-proof weapon which melts once it kills
while (ha!) down here where we chosen bask

in kindlier weathers, with lucky toeholds
    on precincts made safe from intense foul play,
there's no pursuit needs improving much

as the big pomposo clouds roll in
    while fruit trees yield like affable uncles
and Eleanora unbuttons her shirt.

"Who's Eleanora?" Gloria asked even then, when Andrew had finished reading aloud this bit of precocious deconstructivism. The tiniest tinge of spittle appeared at the edge of her full lips.

"Poetic license," murmured Andrew, eyes downcast.

"Ha ha. Very ha," replied Gloria in her projective voice.

Nothing had yet occurred of significance between the two of them, at least as far as I knew, yet already she seemed mildly pissed at his making poetic reference to an invented lady.

"I love that poem," I threw in. "So hoveringly incomprehensible." Yes, instinctive young chap that I was, from the start I'd courted Andrew with praise, and plain to see, he was already mine.

I don't indulge in that sort of seductive maneuver any more, of course. Quite the contrary. But back then....

6.

After the meeting where we'd plunged for the all-Andrew issue, flushed, excited, first devoting an hour to shooting out reject-slips to other potential contributors, we went for a beer, but instead jumped in to the art movie playing at the Bijou across the street from our local. Wednesday afternoons at the Bijou were devoted to classics, this time ECSTACY with Hedy Lamarr, that lovely's first film, notorious for its nudity far ahead of its time, Hedy romping through a forest, for example, whose birch trees functioned as fig leaves though which her fine breasts remained coyly on display.

Now here's a footnote to relish: in deference to Midwestern values, the film's exhibitor had arranged a doctored version by x-ing out Hedy's nipples whenever — as frequently — they appeared. This created an astonishing effect. The actress leapt and raced about in a dazzle of X's that kept the eyes mesmerized by the very feature they attempted to excise. Her breasts, stroboscopically accented by X's, emitted dazzles of light.

Our laughter about the nipple-effect was infectious, the mood ripe with jollity as the three of us — Mamoolian had a home life to attend to — moved on to drinks and supper and then parted to follow our separate ways. One didn't usually move in with one's girl in that conservative neighborhood in those days, plus Gloria and I had worked out a schedule preserving autonomy, with her sleeping over Saturday nights at my place on Stewart Circle and me in her ample, parent-subsidized third floor flat every Thursday on Hoover Memorial Boulevard. This was a no-action Wednesday, already 10 p.m. What moved me to knock at Andrew's dorm room at such an hour? Some premonition, perhaps, disguised as an editorial question about one of his poems. In any case I knocked. And in every way, pretty Zizzic was there.

7.

Discovering her unclothed with Andrew came as a blow whose aftershocks I can still access fifty years later. In the movie version of what happened next my character would have rushed right in and caused havoc. But we all know such dramas rarely occur in actual life. That's why we have movies, stories, art. Anyway, Andrew confronted me at his door, blocking my way, noting that he was just turning in, could it wait till morning? Then, over his shoulder (where could she hide in that tiny room?) I caught a glimpse of my darling, arms crossed to conceal her opulent breasts, cowering in the far corner beside the bed, a dark triangle I knew well (and much admired) left oddly exposed.

Civil for the moment, I pretended not to see — I begged Andrew's pardon for the imposition of my 10 p.m. presence, tomorrow would do just fine — AND SUDDENLY up came Mr. Hyde: I shoved Andy, I stumbled in. Gloria screamed and one hand raced down to the triangle while the other arm womanfully strived to make the vision of Eve in the Dorm Room acceptable as polite portraiture.

"Don't you dare hit him!" she cried, in reference to my considerable bulk in comparison to slightly built Andrew in his once-white shaggy bathrobe.

8.

So...I didn't pummel Andrew, nor did he surprise me, say, with a fierce response, get the better of me, pictures clattering off the walls as we lurched struggling this way and that, and certainly naked Gloria failed to leap into the fray, never jumping on my back to bring me to the floor to protect her new bed-toy, but hell, maybe in fantasy we can even give her a knife, an ice dagger that she plunges into me, it punctures my left lung, I'm writhing on the hook-rug as they look down at my throes in astonishment while I make truly horrific sounds like a bag-piper out of control.

No, as reported, all remained more or less civilized. I stood in mid-room, silent, miserable, as Zizzic found her discarded clothing to cover her astonishing nakedness. Hurriedly she dressed, even slipped into her black leather boots. Andrew kept saying "I'm sorry, I'm sorry, everything started happening so fast. It was Hedy Lamarr's fault. I regret this, Elton, more than I could possibly say."

"Then shut up, don't say. She's free and Jewish and 24, she can do whatever she likes, she doesn't *belong* to me, that's pretty obvious, isn't it?"

"But you must know that nothing untoward occurred," Andrew said. "I...we do owe you an explanation, Elton." This he added as I slumped down on the one chair in the room, an arm cast across my reddened eyes, a concealing arm, like Gloria's across her breasts.

9.

They explained that It had been "an experiment." He'd revealed to her that he'd been baffled for years about the nature of his sexuality, riotously interested yet somehow unable to perform. Not that he felt yearnings for men, he didn't think so, only experienced a degree of blocked closure with women. He had never had more than a glimpse of any teasing female body features via unguarded instants with his mother and three sisters, so the Zizzic agreed to play Hedy Lamarr for him, to give him the visual experience of female gifts at full barrel — so he could check it out, you understand: would he be stirred beyond his damned nuanced complexity of feeling and aspiration? This to clarify future seekings, not with her, not with Gloria, she was my girl, they both remained entirely clear about that.

Reader, you've already been reminded of how the me-back-then reacted in arranging a whacky display of my rival's equipment. I guess this was with an old-brain hope of showing her how he drooped compared to my more or less permanent hard-on. Meanwhile I felt as if the whole center section of my anatomy had been pummeled into a thin, fiery seethe, as if raging oceans of eels mixed with swirling gravel sluiced through me. Certain discoveries, injuries, result in images that will be taken up and renewed in consciousness over and over while never losing their force. If I've used rather light language in recounting this situation with Gloria and Andrew, it's only to reach for a more weathered perspective. I was hurt, sure, harmed, but my first instinct — why is that? — was to conceal the extent of my trouble, to react casually. Betrayal has always gotten to me big time. The story they offered actually caused me to pause, tempted, pussy that I was, to settle for such an improbable account. But there also arose a smell, a savor in that little room. I glanced about and realized I was searching for a discarded condom.

"Take off that robe, Andrew!"

26

10.

Gloria followed me out of Andrew's room and he rushed after me as well, re-robed. "Wait, wait," they called, but I was off along the corridor, none too stable in my feelings, down the stairway as if over a cliff, tumbling into the quad where the late September wind blustered and shoved. You'd need info on Zizzic — *"Who was she / That all our swains commend her?"* — and some background on my own endemic Jewish watchfulness to fully understand the emotional components of this showdown. I refer to a certain brand of paranoia and the way it leads to variations on stiff-necked pride, an unfortunate trait often seen as characteristic of my tribe.

Are there those who feel at ease with the world as it does its job on them? I imagine so. Members of dominant groups, entrenched adherents of religions and cults, the lucky young in first love. But surely for many, if not often reported due to the unsavory tang to such talk, there's literal fear every day, dread of being misused, unjustly treated, outright abused. Why else would the arts of the world offer so many safely vicarious ways to experience terror? For a minority member in a violent neighborhood, for a woman in danger of becoming prey, for a Jew brought up on anxiety in a depression era household, special claims of justification may be made. Those who seem neurotically doomed to expect the worst will have their anticipations confirmed. Which is to blame the victim, of course. On the other hand, many transcend timidity, act "as if" they felt confident while braving the daily labyrinth, and this has always been my way. But I don't want to conclude a sad side note with a self-indulgent "woe is me" riff, so I'll add one of my own Andy-influenced poems from FORGET YOU!, my 1997 new-and-selected, to put a somewhat playful coda to a psychologizing detour.

27

SEXY DAYS

Remember back in sexy days with all those
nutty ways we'd cover our ears?

Mostly via hair-style, of course, but remember Cuties
who drove us crazy flashing actual ear-holes?

Oh to catch a glimpse of naked ears by starlight,
we youngsters rubbing ears in a park at broad noon,

the shameless flaunting, the lobe-enlargements,
the feathers and dangles and everyone twitching their ears!

11.

Gloria Zizzic first said hello to me as I walked through Latimer
Park one day. She sat on a swing, alone on a children's swing-set.
That's all she said: "hello," not with any particular intent or force
to her tone, but with enough of a lilt and glint of eye to cause me
to stop in my amble toward the White Cloud Laundromat, lug-
ging my pillowcase stuffed with washable clothes.

I wandered closer. "Do we know each other?"

"Not yet," said Gloria.

You remember words like that.

We wound up at the White Cloud together. She said she liked
to watch the dryers as they spun their various intimate oscilla-
tions of cloth.

What did she look like? In my tribe we call such females *zoftig*,
substantial. A lot of substance to Gloria, all nicely proportioned,
her face rather cute, kewpie-doll-ish, round, earth-mother-Great-
Queen style, full lips, dark eyes, nearly Frieda-like brows.

The White Cloud provided a set of vending machines. I bought her a hot chocolate and for me a coffee, these in paper cups. I also invested in peanuts and potato chips.

We sat watching the dryers do their riot of display

"So," she offered, "you're not from around here, I gather. And you wear boxers, imagine!"

I could already sense that I was vastly over-matched.

"Linden, New Jersey," I told her, "then off to Storrs as an undergrad, mostly fooling around." I ignored the snide comment on my taste in underwear, though I did switch to briefs as of my next purchase, and have been with them ever since.

"Tell me a funny Storrs story. Or a Linden. C'mon. We have to defend against boredom, which is a widely recognized poison."

"I agree. A story from Storrs. No wait, from New Jersey."

"For starters. But stand up and do it right. From the heart. Think of me as a massive screaming audience at Madison Square Garden."

"You don't look like a massive screaming audience, Gloria."

"How *do* I look?"

"Very pretty."

"Oh, that's good — a guy who understands women."

"In fact, you're as pretty as a kumquat, as pretty as a —"

" — vegetarian?"

"I wouldn't go that far."

We paused and sort of gazed at one another with fatuous smiles, since what was happening felt like the best life has to offer.

Recollecting ourselves, we sobered: "So," she asked, "you teaching English 10s? I've seen you around. Your kids stay awake in class? I keep feeling that mine are waiting for me to break into song, like 'Come to Me My Melancholy Baby'."

It took me this long to notice that more than one toiling house-wife in the place so well stocked with bawling babies was listening in. We were, after all, a handsome pair, and clearly already "into" one another, as one would put it these days. Afterwards we went back to her flat — this was in the autumn of the year before Andrew — and made out on her beautiful brass-framed bed.

It didn't surprise me that she liked to be on top.

12.

I think Gloria chose me for my height and my brawn, for this was a girl rising up to five eleven herself, her height a problem for her all her life. I actually had two full inches on her, not to mention seventy pounds and counting, so there was that. But maybe she also went for me because of the safety feature of my Jewishness, which on some level must have created a homey appeal. Is it a universal law that one either leaps wildly toward Otherness in partner-seeking or stays cozily close to home? This was before I'd met her father, of course, a pushy, suavely dark force of nature whom I faced as if looking into a funhouse mirror. He saw it too, with a brief smirk, her choice of me understood as a complement to his own swarthy power over her imagination, for I might have taken the same lawyer-on-the-left route as his if writing hadn't claimed me, teaching as my day-job at various campuses that I once called labyrinths without Minotaurs.

The sex at that early stage in my involvement with Gloria was, to put it exactingly, *water-buffalo*.

"Whoa!" she said when we concluded for the first time in her wonderful bed and fell apart. "Whoa," the very exclamation she was to blurt after first hearing Andrew's poems the following September.

Another of those early poems of Andrew's, this one also untitled:

human males
            rage hot for sex
                        in every season

            pulsing at chilled iron gates
    closely locked till spring

        so my rollicking mates and I,
    we called them,
                        "great women," the girls
        who said yes...

                each time it seemed a miracle
        (who knew what urged them?)

                that small
                        whispered word
        entered us
                and exploded.

Come to think of it, how could an Andrew who'd written such a poem get away with the hokey claim that all he'd wanted was a view of Gloria's charms, to set his bewildered erotic feelings into focus?

13.

For days after the encounter in the dorm room I ignored her, or let's say we ignored one another. I simply did not turn up for our Thursday assignation and without surprise she failed to show at my place on Saturday.

31

Were we about to leave it at that, after a year in one another's lives and arms, ending our thing with an unmediated, undiscussed withdrawal?

Hardly.

Sundays, every now and then, I would take my puttering old Studebaker out for an airing to keep the battery alive, drive the thirty-some miles to the nearby major city, one that had all the sophistication of, say, Indianapolis, and make my way to the single authentic deli within 600 miles. Lox, cream cheese, bagels, a rare bonanza. I badly needed gustatory consolation that morning. I drove slowly, for my eyes insisted on clouding up with sorrow over flashes of Andrew's blue speedo, Zizzic's luscious face, breasts, triangle, betrayal, betrayal.

I reached the deli on West 4th Street about 10:30, accumulated my locally rare yummies, sat in the car staring blankly ahead at the obscene phallic monument marking the center of town, a civic gesture to those lost on both sides during the Civil War. When I got back, just a few blocks from my own place, I saw her at the side of the road, very serious-looking. She stood there proposing a hitchhiker's gesture, thumb cocked out in my direction. At first she seemed an apparition. Had she instinctively expected me to pass that way? And then I realized she would have found my car gone from its spot in back and put this together with my ethnic Sunday food-urgency.

Her expression was Amazonian-grim, her thumb thrust stiffly, not vibrating, and she wore, I realized with sinking heart, more or less the same clothes she'd tumbled back into on Wednesday with A.N.

I stopped. She entered the car. No words between us. I pulled up and parked in back. We sat there for what seemed a lifetime, likely five seconds.

"Can I have some, too?" she asked in her smallest voice, gesturing toward the deli brown bag with its ravishing scent.

32

14.

Zizzic. What a name. The usual Ellis Island story, grandparents arriving with their four kids as Zizzicowskis, reaching the mainland castrated down to Zizzics.

They'd done the NY Eastside thing, fifth floor tenement, selling from a pickle barrow fourteen hours a day, laundry flying high above the alley, claw foot tub in the kitchen. Gloria's father had the Jewish scholarly gene in spades, he would have cut off both arms if that were required to gain an education. He'd met the Zizzic's Momma while she represented that rare commodity, a woman completing a law degree at NYU.

Job chances took them in a mid-westernly direction, where Gloria and her sister Melinda prospered in their schooling, for give a Jew a book and tomorrow-the-world. I myself have never had protection against the appeal of gorgeous blonde non-ethnics, but for going deep and staying the course? Such a connection required a girl who might wear glasses in bed, one who returned to her Emma Goldman or Jane Austen after ecstatic completion.

Gloria had a gift I've never encountered in another: she would come instantly, often at times even before penis could achieve full entry. And she'd experience after-shocks, that's what we called them, vibrations zizzing up her body and apparently emerging from the top of her head. These could play through her by the score, until at last, satiated, there would came a still moment with closed eyes before her glasses were resettled for another chapter of Aunt Emma or Aunt Jane.

"Should I take them off?" she asked — of the glasses — early in our collaboration.

"They turn me on," I honestly replied.

33

15.

We shared our lox breakfast in relative silence. She washed the dishes. Then I came up thrustingly behind her at the sink, hands cupping her breasts, my mouth at her neck, why was I acting in this coarse way? I assume mainly out of cruelty and self-assertion. She graced me with the heart-wrench of a sigh.

"Are we over it, then? Do you believe me now? There wasn't..."

"Shhsh, shhsh," I whispered, humping.

"No, let's talk about it." She managed to turn in my arms. "Elton, stop that. Please. I feel just terrible."

A certain brutality of payback had surged through me, which of course she picked up through her fine female psychic nerve ends and deflected into talk. We settled at the little pine table by my sunny window, no curtains, no shade, an open view to the back area with its trash cans, cars, ragged bushes. She had a new idea to offer, but first she told me a story from her girlhood. "I should know better than to share this with you, but it relates to what happened over at Andrew's."

She apparently hadn't reached the "Andy" stage. "Tell," I said. All my effort turned toward remaining calm, unperturbed.

"I went steady once," she said, "back in 11th grade. It was with this lad named Seymour, nice kid, son of friends of my parents, premature 5 o'clock shadow, head of close cut hair you could smooth your fingers across, dark, you know, if that gives you a type. Like you, really. And one day, I can't remember how, I wound up without him at the Youth Center where we'd go mainly to play ping pong. One of Seymour's friends said he wanted to show me something at his house nearby and I went along and we wound up in his room and he made moves on me and I said no, of course, because my heart belonged to Seymour, and so we settled for my bringing him off by hand."

A pause.

"Are you all right with this? What we did was just to sit there side by side on his bed and I stared straight ahead while my left hand..."

"Okay, okay, spare me the details, I get the gist."

"Point is, it didn't seem like such a big deal to me. It was kind of cute, to me, really, a kindness. As I saw it. But when Seymour wanted to know where I'd been..."

"...you told him all about it?"

"Yeah. And now I'm telling you. Is this some kind of a test?"

16.

Well, men and women, *vive la différence*. For the life of her she couldn't understand in more than a surfacey way why her Seymour took the kindness of the stroking hand so hard. The opposite of *hard*, as it happened, for he couldn't get it up in future with baffled Gloria, and in not too long a time they ended their arrangement.

She felt that her so-called "betrayal" of me with Andrew had a similar innocence, if you could only pause to think about it. "Besides," she said, "face the signs, it's you who turns him on, you, you big lug, not me. These dicks! No wonder they call you guys *dicks*. Dicks! Nothing else counts, does it? Look, you're my fella'," she said. "Can't you just forget it? Maybe I was a little high, maybe I just like to show off, okay? Maybe I was Hedy Lamarr. Spend enough time convincing a girl she has to cultivate her assets, leg-shaving, beauty parlor, the shopping, the make-up, the bras and the panties and the coy remarks of course by then you're dying to reveal the actual goodies, let the clothes drop, treat a body as a taunting gift. I should write about this stuff, I really should. Not even Virginia Woolf got into it."

"Pass me one of those macaroons," I told her.

17.

And so we started again with scheduled Thursdays and Saturdays. And admit it, Reader, you're beginning to find these revelations from a far past rather tawdry. Are you mainly judging me, or Zissic, or Andrew? All of us, everyone in sight? Please, hold off a bit, keep that open mind you're famous for, or recall some improbable turn in your own history. I can't leave the gory stuff out if the full story's to be told. My situation was clouded by the fact that nothing would stop repeats of the vision of her cowering unclothed in the far corner of Andrew's room. I'd received a blow to my confidence that evening, but I acted with her as if all had returned to where we'd been before. Our particular era, our 1950's, has been caricatured as prissy, but not so, not if I have anything to say about it. There was Gloria's raging libido to report, and Andrew's ambiguous sexuality to ponder. My solution was to keep carefully away from him. But our little offices in the English Building were only three doors apart. We'd pass in the hall, in the coffee room. For a time our contact consisted of little more than curt nods of recognition, indications that we realized the other existed. Then, one day, both grabbing a coffee between sections of English 10, we found ourselves alone in the lounge with its tiers of cubbies for mail and notices, its worn couches, its low table covered with copies of PMLA, the Times Educational Supplement, the pathetic local newspaper.

"Elton," he stuttered out, "I've got to be straight with you. I'm seeing Gloria."

"What?"

"On Mondays and Tuesdays."

18.

You'll assume that this announcement from Andrew ended things between me and Zissic. Or that I moved against him at last in full violence. But no, what actually happened was...we shared her.

God, that doesn't sound so good.

But it's what we did. According to the two of them, they had no trouble resisting "going all the way," not only as a gesture toward my greater claim but also due to Andrew's various kinks. It was the same story as before. They'd become friends. They found it possible to talk and commune. They liked to snuggle during their special evenings but that was it. They never spent the entire night together — on Andrew's narrow cot, how could they? — she'd be off to her own place. Or so they claimed. But was she naked like before, to stir him up? No response, no clear answer, a matter treated silently, none of my business. And weren't we all opposed to the Midwestern Big Brother Ministry of Anti-Intimate Relations? Didn't I believe that humans, born free, needed to fight to stay that way no matter how brutally prodded by the forces of repression and make-nice? Hadn't I read my William Blake?

If she wanted to fuck Andrew, who could have stopped her? In fact, it turns out that many times she did want exactly that, but Andy's squeamishness stood in the way. Or so I was told. And what if she just liked to show her body? It was *her* body, right? Didn't it belong to her? And didn't I enjoy viewing it too, her glorious body? I'd mooned slavishly enough over what a more decorous age would have called "her charms." Isn't what's good for an Elton good for an Andrew?

The situation had me wildly confused. I didn't know what to feel, how to be.

And so we continued.

It does sound from this as though our threesome consisted of the only thing taking place at the time, but no, other newsworthy items also stirred in 1957. Liz Taylor shifted from one marriage to

another, a brave little black girl and eight friends faced down sla-
vering bigots in Little Rock, Arkansas, and Mario A. Gianini died,
the inventor of the maraschino cherry. (I googled to recapture the
1957 details). Albert Camus won the Nobel Prize in '57, while In
Tulsa, Okalahoma, they buried a brand new Chevy Belvedere in a
time capsule along with some gasoline in case that fuel would have
disappeared from human memory by 2007, which is when the
car and other memorabilia were released from the atomic bomb
proof vault under the lawn of the Tulsa County Courthouse, the
contents found safe from the bomb but the car ruined by water
seepage and having no need for the thoughtfully hoarded gasoline. Oh, and on the very day that Gloria and I got back together,
Saturday October 5th, the once Boston Braves, midwesternized
as Milwaukeeans, tottered along toward their first World Series
win since 1914 — over the Yankees, of all teams, think of that.
We listened to Game Three in the faculty lounge, a wild rout of
the ultimately triumphant Braves who lost that game 12 to 3,
with a guy named Kubek, a Yankee rookie playing left field, the
provider of two home runs, great stuff for a rookie, Kubek eventually declared Rookie of the Year, where is he now? And lest we
forget, the day before Game Three the Soviets scared us shitless
by launching Sputnik and sending our country into an overdrive
of *strive*.

We noted all this and more, of course; we cared, we reacted,
we babbled, we opined; but what went on of central importance
to us was the odd little family of three we'd become.

19.

Gloria had theories. I guess one would have to say she'd turned
out to be ahead of her time. Open a Tulsa bomb-proof capsule
containing the three of us in '57 and — granted the likelihood of
water damage — what you would have found was a set-up that

didn't go down too well in the neighborhood, once our arrangement leaked out. We were deemed irreligious if not worse, legally sanctionable not only at the hands of our pious neighbors but also in the view of many in the English Department, where you'd anticipate more respect for experimentation.

Fifty years after these midwestern days, still as far to the left politically as one could safely go without falling off the planet, Gloria agreed to examine our adventure in an exchange of e-mails. Of course she was Lady Norton by then, a converted Brit, Andrew's knighthood and her attendant promotion to ladyhood she found quite funny, given her anarchic views. The title, she claimed, actually pissed her off, calling into question a life-length commitment to causes antagonistic to the Crown. But she couldn't talk Andrew into refusing the honor, though she did make a point of not attending the ceremony. Andrew, with only his male secretary in attendance, went off to London to visit the Queen, a poor sober woman just doing her duty as folks knelt before her to be exalted by her sword.

One of Gloria's recent e-mails:

> *You were in many ways a shit back then, Elton, but at least you were quick to claim the title for yourself. And also many a time you could be sweet, I'll admit it, and as much as the world hopes to keep its slaves defined and colored within the lines, the three of us did progress a bit further than poor D.H. Lawrence there for a while. We didn't give a flying fuck if what happened in the privacy of our insanity was okay with anybody else. That's something to brag on, come time for settling up.*

She ended this particular e-message in our nostalgic sequence by quoting from a well-known poem of Andrew's, perhaps as a nudge at me to return at last his handwritten originals. I was tempted to give them up, my last connection to our relationship, if only to repay the kindness of her easy tone in the e-exchange.

I read them over, those boyish experiments on coffee stained pages, cheap paper, veering grayward now, and then for comfort read them again in print in the edition of *Sheaves* we'd devoted to Andrew's work. The gift was there, the charm. "Boyish" is the word, both for him and the poems. Lithe, off-hand, timid yet casually daring, poems somehow reflecting the clean, Greek kouroi lines of his body. Gloria always claimed there was an erotic charge between me and A.N. How fiercely we would have scoffed at this back then!

20.

I know I don't cut a very attractive figure in this story. It strikes me that I would come off considerably better — odd how narrative devices acquire a moral dimension — if only one shifted the discourse to a 3rd person point of view.

Example:

Elton Gold in his golden days felt shame at going along with Gloria's cultivation of two lovers at once. Shame, of course, is your great civilizing force; without shame we'd still be flinging our feces about and screaming among the trees. Shame, hence civilization, undeniably a good thing; civilization, hence all our woes.

A man was expected, Elton assumed, to display a disgusted or enraged response to Gloria's Queen Bee freedoms, while in fact he admired her *chutzpah*, she was so fuckin' fearless. She'd inherited from her family a demonstrator's passions, organizing rallies against the death-sentence for the Rosenbergs four years earlier, carrying UMW picket signs in West Virginia with her Marxist Pa and Socialist Ma when she was no more than ten years of age. She had *views* and damned if she'd let them be compromised by the narrow, repressed time-serving mentalities around her.

Elton had no need to be taught by Gloria that there were cultures where polymorphic sexuality served as a norm. In Tibet, brothers shared wives. In the Samoan Islands...but you know all about that. Plus there'd always been women throughout history whose energies consumed squads of lovers, unwilling to adopt, in Gloria's words, "an emotional set of iron shackles convenient for social control." And then there was the other side of the Great Divide, the way eros surged among men: their harems, their dependence on prostitution, pornography, the cheating husband syndrome. Where was it written, Elton jotted in his notebook, that one could only have one beloved? Well, in the Bible, he guessed. Where was it a requirement to respond violently to a lady's other guy or else be thought despicably weak in the absence of rage? In the army he'd encountered a revealing twitchiness dominating male sex talk. One guy in Korea could always get a laugh with a mocking removal of cunt-hairs from his teeth. The desired military stance seemed to relegate the well-tamed female to literal slavery. One guy said "I want to marry me a good traveling dog." A girl Elton had gone with when he first returned from his army tour told him that her last boyfriend expected her to turn up in his bed-room two blocks away to start his every morning with an obligatory blow-job.

See? Tricky, the way such story-telling can provide a cushion against condemnation. What feels objectionable as self-pleading becomes judicial and explanatory in third person mode. We are creatures composed of words, after all — men and women of letters, so to speak.

21.

Separate nights created separate adventures with Gloria, a don't ask, don't tell arrangement. Instinctively Andrew and I followed an unspoken iron rule: leave the pain at the door, do not finger the wounds. Did the question persist in my mind as to whether Mondays and Tuesdays with Andrew were for fucking as well as for viewing, chatting, snuggling? And such questions remained as unanswered as they were unasked. Both Andrew and I treated as lightly as we could Gloria's rants about freedom and the courage it took to maintain a share of it. Once established, however, our arrangements took on a mind of their own. More and more often my nights with Gloria were filled with nothing but sleep. Our great crusade against monogamy had somehow veered toward the chaste. Was it the same between her and Andrew? No way to find out, given the presence of the silence that was intended to make it all bearable.

But there came times when the three of us were together in public. Say at T.A. meetings. These were held monthly as a department monitoring device. Professor Wedikin, Grad Student advisor, sat at the end of the conference table in 127 Harrap Hall. As to the seating of the odd threesome, well, at the first T.A. meeting we spread out as far from one another as possible. This was in early October. Then, first Friday of November, I arrived a mite late and found the two of them side by side with their clipboards at the ready for receiving academic announcements and teaching wisdoms. The seat to Gloria's left remained open. I settled there. All three of our faces were understandably flushed. What more could be added but Scarlet Letters? I even recall some of the matters officially discussed at this November meeting of the Freshmen Comp teachers, for I'd begun to take daily notes on our situation, hoping to use them to sort out my feelings. In a way, Gloria and I were never closer than in our increasingly a-sexual connubial nights. In her grand bed we'd taken to whispering, as if the room were bugged.

> Whisper to us, Kama, God of Desire,
> no lack,
> for we are the thirst and the drinking,
> the ringing and the bell.
> — *Elton Gold*

22.

When she and I were together, sometimes she just liked to have her mouth on me...at other times — at last — mine on her: that unforgettable taste of musky peaches. She gradually took more and more against "penetration." We discussed none of this, our mute bodies alone seemed to tell us what was called for. Otherwise we'd spend much of our time reading, grading student papers — sharing the kids' more comical phrasings — hitting the movie at the Bijou, the only screen in town. But then, one Saturday, just before dozing off, she asked: "Where are we going with this?"

"With what? With us?"

"Who else? We're the only ones here."

"On Thursdays and Saturdays." I couldn't resist.

"So it's my friend Andy again?"

"Okay. Sure. Where are we going with *that*?"

"Why don't you come over and see? He's up for it. A visit from the Owner. But back to my question. What is this we're having here between you and me, Elton? Are we talking long-term here, or are we just dicking around?"

"You astound me, Gloria. Am I hearing a classic female query from the Great Experimenter? Marriage on your mind now? Plighted troth? Come on!"

"Fuck you, Elton. Which, come to think of it, is about all we've ever done with one another. No, I don't want to marry you, God forbid. I just want to *talk about it.*"

"So talk already. I'm in favor of talk. Only I thought talk made you feel judged? That's not fair, by the way, what you said about the-only-thing-we-ever-do."

"What else?"

"We *talk,* bitch! We eat. We go to movies. We grade each other's fucking Freshman *themes!*"

23.

Hard to believe, looking back, but I did take up her invitation to visit at her place during one of their nights. Her flat, subsidized by the doting parents, was decorated in a style we'd later learn to call retro. Peacock feathers. Raffia chairs with grand curving backs. The famous brass bed. Curtains of paisley cotton, valenced neatly at the top.

As with Gloria herself, the apartment oddly combined the anarchic with the respectable. She had a little study formed out of a former clothes closet providing just enough room for a desk made of saw-horses supporting an unpainted plywood top at which she'd sit in proper posture in what we called a lady's chair, a slight, gold-lacquered thing with damask upholstered seat suited for decorative purposes in a white and gold boudoir, hardly a substantial perch for a woman built like Gloria. She had narrow plank book shelves climbing near to the ceiling, held up by black screwed-in shelf hangers and filled to bulging mainly with classic and feminist texts. The small sitting room held those insane fold-out "captain's chairs" ubiquitous at the time, also many cushions and one orange burlap covered sandbag-thing. And everywhere were stand-up lamps with triple black bulb holders. You'd have to call the furnishings grad-student-moderne, hand-me-downs from home. But the bedroom where we gathered as often as in the homey kitchen with its one old brick wall that moved us particularly, the bedroom was full retro country, peacock country, festooned with lacy curtains, a Samara rug, the big bed, the turntable and speakers on the long white dresser with its golden dragon knobs.

As a visitor that momentous Monday I sat on the boudoir chair, mate to the one Gloria used in her closet study. Andrew started out on the bed, but after a while he settled on the rug, leaning against the bed end.

"Feels like the showdown," he said, "at Bar B Corral."

Gloria giggled and I of course scowled. Andrew lit one of his tiny Wills Wild Woodbine cigarettes out of a diminishing supply brought from the old country. He smoked with insouciance, an elegant dip at the wrist.

"Listen you guys" — Gloria broke the ensuing silence — "do we really have to get into heavy discussion mode? I see that's where we're headed."

"Sure," I said, "can't we just fuck and be happy?"

"Right to the point as always," said Andrew.

"What are we doing with this, this situation, really?"

"You should know, Ms. Kali, it's nothing if not about you." Spoken in my calmly measured tones.

Play the rest as a *movie-scene:*

GLORIA
Why must The Woman forever be the
Playmaker?

45

ANDREW
For that she beareth the keys to the Kingdom.

ELTON
For that she be-eth the Protectress of the Moat.

ANDREW
Please let us not forget the Portcullis of the Castle.

GLORIA
Oh guys, come on. Let's just have a hug and stop
the cuteness. Let's just not say anything for a while?

24.

At first, what came next was purely twitchy and self-conscious, namely the addition of family nights (Wednesdays) to our schedule. It wasn't as if Andrew and I could imagine taking an observer's role as the other performed in carnal worship of the Zizzic, so mainly Wednesdays were talk, or we'd go out to a bar, or out for a burger and maybe just to wander about from the bedraggled lots on the bedraggled river up through the string of stores along Bradley Boulevard, the main drag of the town. Once, on impulse, we paused at the window of Mr. Garis's Cutatorium with its posters and window-chalked prices and damned if the Zissic didn't opt for short hair right then and there while A.N. and I sat around with the sports and funny papers making our Elton and Andrew "funny" comments and she came out of the experience looking more like Betty Boop than she might have anticipated. "Is okay?" she kept asking, flouncing what the barber had left of her crowning glory. Mr. Garis's offered words consoled her somewhat, our more elaborate reassurances brushed aside.

"It'll grow back," Mr. Garis had said.

And it did.

25.

Memories. There were times of manic laughter. Once, given the sort of Kama Sutra reading we'd gotten into, Andrew was discoursing about how what kept him vital was raising Kundalini, and Gloria misheard the word as "cunnilingi," so that got us going with images of the poor guy servicing women, walk-ins welcome. "When you enter Andrew's Cunnilingi Parlor, there's a line-up of the males and a couple girl practitioners for quirky participants, and lady-customers had to choose, just like at an old fashioned brothel, but here the attraction was how the Lingus-tricks stuck out their vibrating tongues." Or: "Just a minute, Miss Voss, can I put you on hold? I have to finish off Mrs. Robinson over here."

We thought such stuff was truly funny.

26.

Meanwhile, of course, the teaching continued for the three of us, and at our jobs we maintained straight-faces. The way it worked, the English Department had a large lecture meeting for all the composition students once a week, Dr. Geuss discoursing on such matters as openings and closings, Introductions, Bodies, and Conclusions. Attendance at these lectures was required of T.A.s as well as of our students, and best for us to pretend to take notes as the old bird rambled on. Our threesome by then sat cozily together, Gloria in the middle. We'd pass notes on tiny slips of torn off tablet paper to keep ourselves awake. Sometimes these would look like fragmentary poems. I collected as many as I could, for I enjoyed their dashed-off silliness, though some got crumpled up and tossed to the floor of the lecture room.

Perhaps these throw-aways helped eventually to rat us out, like one I remember written by Gloria in her prim penwomanship: "manipulating my two boys, / prop-plane to the left / prop-plane to the right / I could fly all night." She always signed her name to her not-all-that-inspired offerings, and a comic copyright symbol. I'd scribble little sillies like: "Dr. Williams, I'm a twisted arrow / Come cart me off in your l'il old red wheelbarrow." But Andrew might compose at length, as if he were taking Dr. Geuss's gassings down word for word, and the result usually received a covert "whoa" out of Gloria when he passed the fragment along.

> O Great Wisdom Teacher,
> I will do as you say,
> I will memorize the 27 cunning prepositions,
> I will check my spelling twice
> will write profusely from my youthy life
> and in each little dull paragraph
> I will lie that nobody anywhere
> is bleeding.

27.

Most likely something that Mamoolian let slip at a faculty meeting or schmoozing in the hallways did us in. The first sign came from three chirpy folded notes on blue paper addressed to each of us (identical, we compared) inserted in our mailbox cubbies:

Dear Teaching Assistant (You know Who you Are):

The Chairman would like to consult with you. Please indicate when you are free next week for a bit of a chat.

(Uh-oh!)

Molly

Molly was everybody's favorite on the office staff, an earth-momma in muumuus who did everything necessary regarding administration and was a hugger, a species little known in the neighborhood back then.

The Chair. A chat with the Chair.

Uh-oh.

28.

But this meeting with The Chair never occurred, our "case" being elevated to the attention of the Dean himself. November's leaves still tumbled, little redolent smoke-piles in the gutters, the skies dark through the later hours of the day. Before I move on to the encounter with Dean Silver, I feel I've stinted exactly what went on during scheduled encounters with Gloria, both emotionally and physically. Easier to report on the emotional side, but there's always a certain squeamishness as to how the physical gyrations took place. It wasn't as if we spent all that much time actually "doing it," as the pornography industry wants us all to believe, though who knows what style Andy and Gloria followed during their private days. She and I continued in our mock-wrestling way. Laughter could destroy the chances for coupling at any point. Much was done with the mouth, even an amount of spanking occurred — an amazement to me that she went for that, emitting a telling little gasp the first time I risked it experimentally. As to formal fucking, she'd usually post above me. Then back to talk about our classes, our students, back to cooking supper or back to reading, the sexiest activity of all.

When the three of us met together on Wednesdays, things

could still get tense. Gloria would as a matter of course take the middle position on the bed, just wide enough to accommodate so much human freight. At times either Andrew or I grew uncomfortable trying to sleep in the areas left to us so we'd decamp to the couch or gather up cushions and use the floor. But there were other times, like her continued efforts to get Andrew and me engaged with one another. This would happen most often when we were in what had become a characteristic posture, Gloria holding each of our pricks at once, not stroking, just a firm grip. A very special buzz resulted from that, a kind of three-part transfusion as we silently listened to jazz.

At times she'd try to substitute our hands for hers, which didn't work. "Come on, guys," she'd say, "what's the hang-up?" Which leads me back to the emotional side of things. Once, at her urging, I found myself lying half atop frail Andrew, worrying that my weight might snuff the breath out of him, and briefly, as if by accident, we kissed. And then, by God, we both fell to weeping in a rather wrenching way.

He tasted like Wills Wild Woodbines.

Gloria seemed entranced by this.

As to how the extraneous male conducted himself when actual full-Gloria contact took place? From the very first the unspoken rule emerged that the third wheel would withdraw to her living room. Seeing nothing. Hearing everything.

29.

Emotions. Probably not what you'd expect. We grew very close. When the subject came up as to the scheduling of our weeks, with Andrew-Gloria on Mondays and Tuesdays, Elton-Gloria Thursdays and Saturdays. Friday and Sunday set aside as time-outs for solitude, recovery, regret, anticipation, Wednesdays for the always unanticipatible gathering of the full clan, we wondered if we shouldn't shift the schedule around to allow the three of us more time to hang out together.

Gradually this happened, a new agenda emerged: Monday evolved into a threesome evening. Tuesday was sacred to Andrew. Wednesday, threesome, Thursday Elton. Friday quiet time. Saturday threesome. Sunday day of rest. The days blurred.

Were we enjoying this? I can't speak for Andrew, and certainly not for our Dark Lady, but I ached in solitude from the thought of the two of them involved in who knew what. Only wait. One could always peek through the pin-prick hole in Andrew's curtained experience by contemplating the writing he did at the time. Would he allow me to see these poems? No, of course not. But she did.

> naturally naked:
>> cats,
>> birds,
>> bananafish

> & we
> covered creatures
>> who yearn to uncover
>> be uncovered

> men's love songs:
> thin flute fortitude
> despite blind monkeys
>> at the kettledrums
>>> of the mind

> women's love songs:
> volcanic rage
>> intent on ease
>>> and gentleness

51

From way back, because of his early discovery of experimental Americans like Spicer and Brautigan, Berryman, Ishmael Reed, Andrew wrote like no other Brit of his generation, a young man seemingly shy and unassertive, set free when gripped by Gloria, our Muse.

30.

The Dean called us in one at a time.

Sitting in his reception area, its ornate railing before the secretary's desk like a courtroom barrier, we couldn't help but break out in smiles, especially if we happened to glance at the framed likenesses of previous holders of this august office, some dating back to the period of steel-framed eyeglasses and Van Dyke beards.

In a sense we felt like children called up on an infraction, maintaining solidarity against the stuffy big people about to bawl us out.

Andrew was ushered in first. I tried to grip Gloria's hand covertly — as a little joke about our jeopardy — but she pulled away, staring straight ahead. Only then did I realize that she was steaming with righteousness.

It seemed to take eons before A.N. emerged, shaking his head broadly. I motioned him over for a report but he waved me off and pressed through the tall, heavy doors guarding the sanctity of the office.

Gloria's turn came next. And not too long into whatever occurred in there, with a loud F-word fricative, she emerged from the inner sanctum and whooshed through the exit as Andrew had done. By then I found myself fairly shaken. And was called in.

Dean Silver had the hair to go with his name. And a silvery glint to his glasses, plus a Yalie tie, a Brooks Brothers suit that had seen spiffier days, charcoal, striped, with a vest that displayed a watch chain, as if he were sitting for a Norman Rockwell cover for The Saturday Evening Post.

"Mr. Gold."

He offered a nod, glancing up from a dossier on his desk. Quite formal.

"Dean Silver," I returned in kind.

"Would you have a seat, sir?"

The "sir" seemed a bit excessive, but I let that pass. Fact is, I was feeling a bit dizzy, needed a seat, settled before his desk. Was the floor slanted upward in his favor? I felt very small.

"Mr. Gold, I've discussed this unfortunate matter with your friends, as you know."

I should have said, to ramp up my courage, "what *unfortunate matter*?" but I sat there instead and took it.

"Mr. Gold, we've had only the best reports on your teaching, but rumors about...about your private life, you and your friends... we have disturbed students on our hands, I must tell you, and by extension, in a few cases, parents...."

I found my voice. "With respect," I interrupted, hearing a distinctly British tang to my words, as if I had arisen in full wigged regalia to address the bench at the Old Bailey, "I'm unclear as to what you have in mind."

He gave me a long, appraising stare. Then: "Come, come, my boy, no need for that. Let's be men about this and speak squarely."

Though so much slighter in build, he seemed at that point a ringer for Teddy Roosevelt.

"Our problem, Gold" — note the "our," and the familiar yet distancing use of my name — "our problem centers not so much on student concerns, which are essentially friendly to your situation…but we must keep the parents in mind. The parents. And there's an instance where the family contacted a representative in the House of Representatives." With a little dry chuckle: "The *national* House of Representatives."

I decided it wouldn't help to play entirely dumb. Racing through my mind was a set of alternative approaches: outright denial wouldn't cut it, but how about privacy claims? I settled for "What, exactly, am I being accused of?"

"Ah," said the Dean, coming from behind his desk to appropriate the adjoining round-back chair facing mine in all its leathern upholstery and hammered brass fittings, "hmmm, yes, how would you put it yourself, my boy?"

Question answering question, an invitation to self-incrimination, the little seasoning of concern as if veering toward my side of the issue with the shift of seating and the "my boy" stuff.

My instinct also was to shift ground. "What did my friends say?"

"Miss Zissic, I'm afraid," he replied immediately, as if without calculation, "essentially said nothing at all, granted a moment of rather shocking profanity. She simply walked out on me." He actually grinned. "Quite a lady."

"Yes." Pause. "And Mr. Norton?"

"Ah, Mr. Norton. Mr. Norton, I'm afraid, wept."

"He did?" I was surprised. Such intensity of response from Andrew altered my sense of his sophistication and cynic *savoir faire*.

"He fears the loss of his fellowship," the Dean reported sadly.

It came to me to play tough. "Whyever could that happen?"

"You must take this seriously, Gold. What exactly are the three of you up to?"

"If you have to ask, what's this inquest about?"

"About your cohabiting, of course."

"There's a midwestern law against cohabitating?"

"A law? I'm not sure. Surely not, not in so many words. Not

specifically, no. But law off to the side, there've been complaints, the students, some are giddy with it, and certain parents have contacted us, and as I said..."

"...the House of Representatives."

"It must stop, Elton. It just must stop. Whatever it is."

"What it is just happens to be nobody's business, Dean Silver. Privacy. Remember privacy? There's a law about that too."

"I wouldn't bet on it."

I reached the Dean's office door to get out of there but he had something more to ask: "Tell me — how do you arrange it when the three of you...when matters became...?"

I looked back at him across the long room with its worn but good Persian carpet, its polished bronze sconces, the tooled-leather desk and chairs. He was the cleanest, most white-shirted, most rep tie wearing man I would ever see in a lifetime. The very glints from his glasses....

"It's too horrible to contemplate, Dean Silver. Dogs mating on the streets. Horses in the fields. It must be eradicated at the root."

32.

That was the weekend of the local county's Harvest Fair, and we three attended, gawking at the 4-H contest winners, at the triumphant squash and wooly sheep and peach preserves displayed on card tables or in enclosures, with triumph-ribbons of varied colors intensifying it all. They had a little midway with games of skill and chance, seedy to look at, and off at a small distance — with a sign warning that no children were allowed beyond a certain point — a tent drew a waiting line, men exclusively.

Gloria, being Gloria, naturally wanted to join that line. Andrew and I tried to explain as diplomatically as possible that women weren't...

"I'm not a complete idiot, cohorts, damn you. There's some

poor girl in there doing God knows what to give these Blueballs a ride."

No sooner did we attach ourselves to the line than a ripple of unease vibrated through the other prospective customers. A man in a sheepskin vest and wool cap just ahead of us turned full round to observe this tall, fierce-looking women with two young men about to pay to enter the sex-pit tent ahead.

"Not for ladies," he said. Others, too, turned to watch, farther toward the entrance guarded by a man in a straw boater collecting quarters for admission — bulbous nose and megaphonic voice out of W.C. Fields

"Well ain't that a thing," said Gloria. "I'm no lady, mister. Mind your business. Our money's just as good as yours."

This was the first and only time I'd heard Gloria speak Midwestern. The protester spun on his heel, gazed ahead again. Then he left the line altogether.

"Couldn't take it, eh?" said Gloria. "Not used to backtalk."

"Screw you, lady," said the man rather quietly, passing by.

"Oh," Gloria told him, "me and my boys, we've got that covered already, thanks."

Next came our encounter with W.C. Fields. "This is only for the gentlemen, thank you, dearie." He tried to herd me and Andy in and block Gloria's way.

"*Gentlemen* my God!" she said. "Where do you get off preventing a U.S. of A. woman from indulging in a little vicarious poon-tang?"

"Sorry, Miss. The rules. No children. Never had a lady before."

"That's a brand new rule you just made up. 'Never had a lady!' Ladies are no good at much anyhow. Try one of us highly trained *hookers*."

He simply stared. Blushed. He'd never had a Gloria before. At last: "Sorry, Miss."

We left.

"This gets me sooo steamed," Gloria complained as we

wandered the grounds. "Was that Dean Silver there in line? Did you see him, with his hand fiddling at his fly?"

An announcement blared news about the weight-pull contest. There were rows of rusting metal folding chairs set up for audience. We snagged seats toward the back. Out on the field two tractors at a time dragged sleds filled with great boulders. The machines strained at their loads. The contests were timed by stop-watch.

"What are we going to do?" asked Andrew.

"How about we *sue*?" said Gloria.

Andrew and I smiled broadly.

"I'm serious," she said.

"We haven't been arrested yet, Sweetums," I told her. "They were just sending a shot across the bow."

"We're gonna sue! They can't bully us like that!"

"I don't really want to get in trouble with my fellowship," said Andrew, glancing at us shamefacedly.

"Fuck your fellowship and the mule it rode in on. These people are not going to push us around."

"Right," I cried, holding back an affectionate laugh but moved by her fortitude. "Let's shove it in their faces."

"Elton!" said Andrew, "Watch your figure of speech!"

So then we were all three laughing again. We wound up drinking at our local, as so often. I put an arm around Gloria's waist on one side, Andrew's arm around her shoulder from the other. Our three small black sweating glasses of Guinness made connected rings on the table before us.

33.

Recounting our story over such a distance of years has had a therapeutic effect on me. I look back with pleasure on the fact that we decided to go on exactly as before. See, we were angry, cocky, invested; we thought we'd show them, make a point, stretch the boundaries of automatic emotions like jealousy and possessiveness. Ten years later our arrogance wouldn't have seemed quite so maverick (in large cities, anyway) and certainly less unacceptable. My thought is that we all three had an outsider-syndrome working in us long before we became entangled, an alienation that caused the entanglement in the first place. There's a term psychologists like to use: "exceptions." It's a nice way to refer to quasi-borderline personalities. On a scale from straight-arrow-citizens on one end to out and out sociopaths at the other, we were positioned at least a bit off toward the criminal side. There's that poem of Andrew's about the tempting pear dangling over the precipice with all the dragons of hell roaring up beneath with their slimy teeth, and those humans who stretch for the tantalizing pear impossibly high above them, those in that long line of leaper/plungers, remain undeterred by the screams of the fallen mangled by the dragons below.

34.

Of course Gloria's lawyer father got involved immediately once we were fired (officially, "terminated"; cause: "moral turpitude") and thus began the final stage of our journey.

Saul Zissic was the sort of man who would stir up into a rage at any hint of injustice. In criminal defense practice they called him The Badger. Stay away from his burrow, for once he gets hold of you he never lets go.

We were about to become *a cause*. Andrew caught our mood at the time.

> Note the Goddess-smile
> on this insanely gifted girl
> admired by a street-singer as she moves along.

Does this dear person
with her upwardly mobile nipples
her soul brightened by lust and fabrication
wonder if time's come round again
for another Mary?

O, do not blaspheme, do not condemn nor
control nor besmirch,
thou ginger, thou cruel!

she holds her men to her heart

our breasts, steel breastplates,

hers the will of hunger
dissolving armor

The comment I most treasure regarding such examples of A.N.'s early work comes from a review by Stan Hollings in Poetry Mag, that the guy was "an Elvis among the ballerinas." The connection is easy to chart between Andy's experiments in language and our sexual carryings-on. I'd say more, but a kind of blush tends to overtake me when I approach critical discourse, as much as when discussing the body's naked particulars. Why must that be? Let me put it this way: as the threesome continued to function, the schedule of our nights broke down and things actually became rather pristine. Yet sometimes we were indeed rowdy, the three of us together, and I shouldn't chicken out from recording some of that. One chosen instance: Gloria got it in her head that she wanted to feel the force of piss blasting into her, so Andrew and I, both game, took turns entering her while consuming glassfuls of water between efforts, yet neither could produce the required spurt, resulting at last in falling-down laughter from all. Now, was that so terrible, Elton? — see, just words. To say the way it was with us still feels like a sort of "coming-out," another instance of the normally unspoken. Once, when we were all three together and I retired to the other room while Andrew and Gloria got going, I peeked (ashamed about it still), viewing through the slightly cracked bedroom door his poet's ardent head between her spread legs — she'd let him go down on her but disallowed me, at least at that point, who knows why?

> no greater pleasure no deeper self-pleasing
> than to cause another's happiness.

> Eat of my body, dear child.

*

> slowly she unclothes herself, the shameless moon,
> her blemished face grown perfect
> in the dark

*

> ultimate music:
> the loved one's piercing cry.

> *(my poem, never published...in the style of A.N.)*

35.

Have you ever had grown people spit at you on the street? Strangers? It made me wonder what they were protecting. Correctitude? People get rigid asserting their right to measure everyone against the grid work of their own commitments. Castrate the monkey! What's that comin' down the road? — why, it's the Spanish

Inquisition!

Gloria's genetic inheritance came clear the minute I made contact with her parents. The first words I heard from her mother were "So here's the poor man in the middle!"

"*I'm* usually the one in the middle, Amanda."

She called her mother Amanda.

And from the father, Saul: "Welcome, Elton. We're going to have to get you a respectable suit and a judge-proof tie."

36.

But it never came to that, never reached a courtroom. We were fired, as expected, especially since the Imp of the Perverse took over and we decided to flaunt our polyandry. Then Saul Zizzic got in there plus the ACLU on privacy grounds, and for a time it looked like we might make a nationally noted case for the right to enjoy a variation on the early Mormons, a girl feeling religiously obligated to cultivate her own chosen "he-rum." However, a settlement turned out to be the way to go. The university had no relevant cause to terminate our contracts mid-term, and Saul got us each $75,000 after his share. This pot of cash turned out to be one of those great good things that come along now and again, and I mean more than just the money, which helped me through a dry season here and there. (Saul supervised my investments for long-term growth). I refer to the end of the degree-seeking part of my academic so-called "career." Forgive me, St. Eudora of Jackson, for I never fail to extol thee though I left my thesis unfinished; others have taken up that good cause.

The consequence for Andrew and Gloria, of course, was that they famously ran off together to the streets of Old Cambridge, where Andrew became a Don a dozen years later, and where the two actually married to celebrate their reaching a settled port after a stormy voyage.

37.

It's not as if Gloria had been my only experience of crazy love, or at least what passes for such when you're still a kid and everything new feels beyond the limits of the most fevered imagining. Eros is everywhere. While still in high school I looked up the word "satyriasis" in the dictionary and figured I'd spotted my problem. Among the addictions it held an ambiguous place, gaining a certain envy as well as, of course, rampant condemnation. A life as a history of girls and then women, surely that's what mine came down to. When Gloria and Andrew ran off to a future across the sea, I wound up teaching at Lansing and sure enough, exhausted and woebegone, went and married just about the most disastrous person fate could have found for me.

Some good, I suppose, came of it. A daughter, my only child. A lot of writing, which won me my long term visiting poet slot at NYU and elsewhere, plus many sprightly, intelligent friends. But Lynn, my first wife, was a tax lawyer, not a lover. I guess that in her order of priorities sex situated itself just above housecleaning and a few notches below the reading of the *New York Times*. She'd defer to my "needs" in a desultory manner. I'd try to seduce other women who came within our ambit, but these tended so to admire Lynn's worldly power and her status as a successful woman in what had been so dominantly a male bastion that the last thought they'd ever have would be to break an unwritten sisterhood contract for the sake of a furtive affair with the oversexed and undernourished husband of a local culture-hero.

This went on for some time, ending, of course, in divorce. I managed to arrange a visiting teaching gig then, through a friend in Kentucky, and that's where the rest of my endless womanizing began.

Ah, the women of Kentucky! I see you smiling there, Reader, and I must accept the fact that such addiction has its comic and unsavory side. A colleague of mine smilingly calls it "The Poet's

Disease." But for me the tale of our threesome remains a particularly serious and central matter, an experience that created in me an effect roughly equivalent to "a systematic derangement of the senses," the sort of thing the boy Rimbaud had in mind in his prescription for the health of the Poet. Rimbaud speaks particularly of "all forms of love, of suffering, of madness"; he offers "unspeakable torment" as the way. One must become "the great invalid, the great criminal, the great accursed."

I quote Rimbaud now strictly in terms of what the Goddess Gloria in all of her avatars had left me as an endowment:

> *When the eternal slavery of Women is destroyed, when she lives for herself and through herself, when man — up till now abominable — will have set her free, she will be a poet as well! Woman will discover the unknown! Will her world of ideas differ from ours? She will discover strange things, unfathomable, repulsive, delightful; we will accept and understand them.*

Let these be the final words I'll set out, dear Reader, from an eros-addicted poet. But I'll add a fragment from a poem of my own that might also serve as a parting note:

> *in the Women's Room*
> *there's a note for him*
> *amid the graffiti:*

RANDOM FUCKER — CHOOSE!

Only there comes an even deeper memory, maybe the start of it all. I'm a few months beyond age eleven, home from school, hanging up my wet jacket, house empty. I go to the tiny kitchen, pour myself a glass of milk. I find a carton of vanilla cookies and snag about three, then wander into the living room, check out a rumpled copy of the local newspaper two days old, cast it aside, mount the stairway to the second floor.

Down the rain-dimmed hallway I spot a section of newspaper edging out of my sister's partially open bedroom door.

As I bend to retrieve the day's sporting news, I tip the door with my shoulder and it swings even farther open into her very feminine bedroom.

And on the bed — there she is, Sister Selma, asleep in her nakedness atop the white bedspread, stretched out in all her seventeen-year-old excellence and glory like an offering on a huge chenille seashell.

I gaze. Thunder sounds and rain comes harder than before. The boy I was then picks up the newspaper and makes his way downstairs.

Settles to read but can't concentrate.

In his imagining, Selma wakes, stirs, notices with confusion that the newspaper she'd thrown down as she went dozing off is not there, gone from the floor where she'd tossed it.

Uh-oh.

I swiftly smooth the paper and move furtively back upstairs.

I settle the paper as exactly possible, right where I'd first found it, and look up to see her fully on display as before.

Beauty.

Is that a tiny, ill-concealed smirk on her lips?

I stand gazing.

And I should add to the dossier as well the time when Andrew lay on his back at my command with his beautifully alert penis on show amid Gloria-laughter.

From one of her recent e-mails:

> You're writing about our days together? Will you publish? Please allow me, if so, a pre-glance? To assure that you've got it right, as of course you no doubt will, scrupulous to the death. All the sordid details.

64

Is this wise? Won't we come off as a bit twee, given the erotic hullabaloo of the moment? Not that I'd ask you for discretion, Elton. I might ask for many things, and do, and have done, but never that.

As for Andrew, nothing came directly from him. And then I was amazed to learn that he'd dedicated what turned out to be his final collection to me, to me "and memory." Only when I'd bought the thing in paperback from British Amazon did I find my name "and memory" starkly there.

Gloria ended her latest e-post by copying these lines from Andrew's book-length poem THE TRACERS:

> *Men have traded fortunes, whole countries,*
> *to gaze upon a brown nipple.*
>
> *Are these not the saints of Eros,*
> *at peace with their religion?*
>
> *All praise to the vertical smile,*
> *to the widening O,*
>
> *to the rose inviting entry*
> *to bloom again.*

Andrew died of prostate cancer, full of honor, beyond pain, two days after I received this message.

I WILL LISTEN

I'll take you just the way you are.

— Billy Joel

THE SIGN, THE FIRST TIME I stopped to read it, I laughed to myself that they'd maybe seen me coming, being I'm the sort of person who surely needs a listener.

This was before I started to find my way again as a singer-song-writer. I'd always played guitar and gigged locally before the army, but I'd lost confidence once I got back, couldn't catch a feel for how to make things happen in the so called "real world." Two Iraqi deployments fucked me up like everybody else, but I vowed to get over it, relax my mind, deny all symptoms that cost me a decent night's sleep. The best I could do for a job was manning a newspaper and candy kiosk in an ancient building in downtown Philadelphia mostly filled with music teachers, cut-rate dentists, that sort of thing. Depressing place. And, for me, no woman in sight.

I wound up writing a pretty good song about that sign. It must have been posted up quite a while before it caught my eye, scotch-taped at the edges, brownish, curled, and the lettering sun-faded. This was the sort of sad store that might make anybody glance away, embarrassed or something. I wouldn't normally spend time looking in a store-front window like that. They had the sign taped to the inside glass. Behind hung a sheet of yellowish plastic to filter out the sunlight, which made the stuff in the window look faded, like one of those old yellowish photographs.

This was a store where they sell elastic stockings and things for invalids, but you could tell it could be a front for something illegal so the owners would just put in any old random merchandise for show. It looked like a second-hand store, like something from somebody's memory. Just inside the entrance were shelves with sex-books and piles of magazines, and in the window they had thongs and leather outfits, the kind of place where you'd go, I'd guess, to get a whip if you tended that way. It could make you sickish to pass the store window with its faded unmoving look like a summer's day when somebody'd died or when a storm was about to come and time seemed to stop and the light took on an eerie quality.

The sign read: "I will listen to anybody without interruption, $15.00 an hour. A kindly ear for your troubles. Enquire within." That part was printed, and underneath in an uneven, childlike looping hand: "Uncle Zostris."

"I Will Listen" turned out to be one of the first of my post-enlistment songs to gain some attention, even a little air play once I got myself together and started on the coffeehouse route again.

> I will listen so you will stay
> And the waves will glisten
> As they carry us away.

New in that North Broad Street neighborhood I'd never thought much about this particular store. I figured it was some kind of a racket or a come-on, maybe a Gypsy bag-game. And although I'm the sort of person who even might be willing to pay somebody to hear me out, still I never expected to find myself inside there, because you tend to close your ears to what seems to be calling to you, from aversion or fear or something. Say you're in a crowded place, like going down in the subway at rush-hour, and a stranger starts calling out your name and you don't conceivably know anybody in that crowd, you get spooked, even tempted to run back up the stairs as if it were your death calling out to you from among those people. The look of this store window and the sign I'm telling you about had that effect on me. I'd just walk past and enter the Olney Station and ride down to Locust Street to this part-time job the V.A. had set up for me because in a way I was still over there, twitchy, didn't believe I could hold down a job with longer hours.

On one side of the store stood a coffee importer's and on the other a cheap jeweler's and then there was a big pharmacy by the subway entrance. It wasn't a totally run-down neighborhood, but pretty run-down. At least I didn't have far to the subway and my room was okay as such things go. I mean it wasn't the sort of area where you'd just casually take a walk late at night, but I'd be in bed reading anyway, my choice recreation. The real point is how I'd pass the store and it would make me feel queer and depressed and then it just sort of blended away and I knew I'd settled into the neighborhood a bit because nothing struck me very much as unusual.

There never seemed to be anybody in the store, as far as you could see through the front window. You couldn't be sure it was even open for business. I'd say to myself, *not me, Uncle Zostris, if you're looking for me you've got a long wait coming.* And yet you're fated to do exactly what you'd never expect, and I actually did go in there and talk to him and that's what I'm getting at — Uncle Zostris.

It was the summer before the spring when they put the extra cops in the subways, awful things were going on down there, well-off people taking taxis in to business. Mainly it was kids going crazy, of course, knifing people or breaking up things in the trains, it could be like a patrol through insurgent territory just to get to work, or like going the wrong way down a one-way street. That summer the subway was a challenge. I even thought of carrying a pocket knife, but then I decided I'd only get in trouble if anything happened and they found a weapon on me. But the point is, I was more than usually jumpy going and coming. I'd get off my shift at 2:15 and I'd have my big meal then to beat the crowds and I'd buy the Philadelphia Bulletin that had started up again and go back to my room and maybe plink around on my banjo, only the day when this happened I'd stopped for a haircut on Market Street so it was approaching four when I hit the subway and the rush had started, nobody standing as yet but the cars full.

I sat in the last car, reading the ads, and I noticed this very flashy dark haired guy get on in a seersucker suit that looked a little small for him and the queer thing was he carried a walking cane. He was a big guy with his hair combed straight back and a superior kind of a smile on him. The cane was like dark-brown bamboo with a diamond-shaped silver top for show, but it wasn't that he could need a cane for his health or anything. At first he stood by the door, and then after a stop with free seats available he sat down across from me and then he got up and settled down again next to the girl at the end and acted like he knew her. She was a pretty secretary-looking girl, her hair short and curved in about her ears. She wore a sleeveless dress with a sweater in her lap and on top of the folded sweater a cakebox from Horn & Hardart's, just an ordinary girl going home from work toward her apartment or something.

You know how noisy it is, I couldn't hear a word, but he was talking to her, and at first she hardly nodded her head but then she looked at him when he said something with his smile coming up very big and he leaned and whispered in her ear and she half-smiled but you could see she wasn't interested from how she sort of gathered herself in, adjusting the cardboard box on her lap, making herself more compact the way women do, pulling into herself away from him.

He didn't say anything for a while. His face sobered. Then he sort of leaned toward her and talked very fast, not smiling. She ignored him completely this time, looking straight ahead. For all I could tell he was known to her, it wasn't like an ordinary try at a pick-up, because usually the girl will never respond or just get up and walk away if she wasn't interested. But it did seem she couldn't wait for her stop, she patted her face with a piece of tissue and put it back in the drawstring handbag she had. At the next stop I heard him say, without looking at her but sitting there spread out — he seemed heavier sitting that way, like an Hawaiian king or something — heard him say "Well you're way off base."

The next stop was mine, and then I noticed she sort of looked around and she got up too and waited at the door. The man still sat there, an odd, kingly smile on him. We pulled into the station, the doors opened, she shot out and I thought how she was doing the clever thing, getting off that train to wait for the next one and be rid of him that way.

"The doors were already closing," I said to Uncle Zostris. "You get the picture? I heard the doors whoosh behind me and it was like a sigh of relief I'd let out myself, but then the doors opened again and I saw that he'd shoved his cane in there against the edging to make the doors split because he came out with the cane held in front of him like this, you follow me?"

I stopped talking for a bit and rubbed my eyes. I was still jumpy, and Uncle Zostris, who was an old black man, maybe Jamaican, threw his head off to the side on his pillow in his rocking chair and sort of smiled and nodded as if he understood, as if to tell me he saw it all coming, only he hadn't said a word, just like the sign promised, he didn't interrupt.

At first it was hard to get started with him. The woman who led me back to his room in the rear of the store, a fat woman with gold in her teeth, all she said was "Uncle can receive you now." She took my money and said she'd buzz when my time was gone. The old man had been asleep in a chair and she shook him and he came awake with his little smile already playing at his Iips, and then she left us and he motioned me to a seat, one of the two straight chairs drawn up facing his rocker. It was a bedroom with a smell of mildew, some holy pictures on the walls. The wallpaper

71

had a print of fox-hunting scenes. I was half afraid to be in there and still shaken by the subway business and wondering why that had hit me so hard and after I got started talking to Uncle about the man and the girl in the subway, you could hear traffic sounds through the walls and the vibration from the subway and people moving around above the ceiling as if there were kids up there running around in circles. I waited to see if he would say "go on" or something or ask what happened next, like that, but he only nodded, his head tilted against the small flowered headrest pillow and I realized for the first time since I'd come in there that he didn't have a single window in that little room.

I said: "Let me get straight what happened." I told him how the girl was starting toward the exit down the platform but it looked like as soon as the train went past she'd stop and sit on a bench and wait for the next one, and then the doors whooshed apart and out he came with his cane in front of him and she gave a kind of start and turned down toward the opposite exit, which was closed.

"Do you fuckin' know where I mean?" I asked Uncle Zostris, but he didn't give any sign.

Are you listening, Mister?

He nodded as before, with the saddest face, though he kept smiling. His face was all lined as if he'd gotten splashed with acid. As he smiled you could see only two tiny front teeth. His color was a kind of yellow and the skin looked in places like scar tissue, only he had a sort of warmth about him, he wasn't upsetting to look at except that he seemed so tired. I guess I wandered off telling him some other things in my life, about my unit and how I was wounded, but then I came back to what had happened in the subway, how I'd been thinking that I had to do something for this girl but I was afraid, and the big man when he walked after her had already given me a strange look and how did I know they weren't friends or that she was in any danger from him and I thought at that point I'd have to get out of there or do something

72

fast because the girl had seen that the other exit was boarded-up and she was coming back toward the dark-haired man looking straight ahead, "*you understand?*" I shouted this at Uncle Zostris, because at that moment it came to me, by something in his face, that he was stone deaf.

It came to me just as I was about to tell him a lie. Was that what made me see he was deaf and couldn't actually hear me? Because in the subway I'd thought up a scheme, how I would speak to the girl as she approached, call her by some name or other, pretend I knew her, maybe she'd catch on and act like we were old friends and shake off this fellow coming after her. I'd even formed words in my mind like "Sheila! — thought I recognized you! How you been? Where you off to?" and so on, hoping she'd register how I was trying to get her out of there.

Which was true, but the rest I only imagined, imagined how I would wait till the man and the girl came up the platform toward me and I would say something like "Why, hello, Sheila," so the man could hear and how she would look at me — this was the lie — look at me and scream, because then there'd be the two of us coming after her, or so she'd think.

That was the lie I was going to tell Uncle Zostris, that she'd screamed when I spoke to her by a made-up name, because none of this happened, because I couldn't get the thought out of my mind that she would scream if I called her Sheila or whatever, and so what I actually did was to stick my hands in my pockets and climb the subway steps and when I looked back I couldn't see either the man or the girl and a train went roaring through and the roar was still in my ears when I came up and entered the store and the woman led me back where Uncle was nodding, nodding in his chair, and I felt the subway vibration and I jumped up and I shouted in his face "You can't hear me! It's just another lost cause!" and a buzzer sounded and I wanted to kill him, I don't know what pushed me that way, I felt like my insides had melted into a kind of hot, yellowy liquid boiling through me and I went

73

for him and only then did his face sort of click shut as if he saw me for the first time, saw that I was enraged, and he pulled a cane out from under the chair and then the woman grabbed me hard from behind. "Crazy," she said, "only crazies come, it's too dangerous for him, he's too old." I didn't struggle, I went all limp as she led me out, but Uncle Zostris, who'd gotten up, limped a step toward me with the woman holding me and I saw that he was enormously tall but crippled and he took a pad of paper and he scrawled on it: "I know you have suffered. Come again."

Later I wrote my "I Will Listen" song out of that, one maybe you've heard. It's already had several covers. The time in the store with Uncle Zostris isn't in the song but in a way it is. The lie is in there, that I saved her from this guy. I don't know, should I be ashamed of that? It's almost like my putting it in a song made it as good as true.

THE UNLIKELY LIFE
OF CRASHAW PIN

Leave nothing of myself in me.
— *Richard Crashaw*

YES, *THAT* NOTORIOUS CRASHAW PIN, playful poet known (and shortly unknown) for winning an improbable prize, then promptly disappearing from human ken, a fate, by the way, entirely my own responsibility, despite idle talk among conspiracy-addled literary historians regarding a possible murder plot and manuscript-theft. No, as Pin I came, as Pin I saw (a little), even conquered (in a way) then more or less disappeared, fully intending both the ecstatic shimmer and the near-invisibility thereafter. I don't even plan to come clear as to whether I am, beyond this moment of language-making, living or dead. It's true that a speaking mouth must breathe, or, to put it more coarsely, that dead men tell no tales, so you might assume I'm still intact here on our astounding earth, still participating. And you might be right. But ah already I sense a groan from Reader as to my weakness for complication. Listen, Smart-Ass, they didn't label us New Metaphysical Poets for nothing! One thing, dead or alive, I remain in hiding. "Crashaw, you rascal, what's this fear of yours that absents you from worldly felicity and flux? Why not stand up proud and tall?" Reader, *please*! My tale is prime witness to the fact that the strivings and accolades of today can spawn the terrors and transformations of tomorrow. Alive or not, I offer in these pages my joys and doubts, my memories, secrets and musings.

Are you interested in a life-changer? Hold a new-born infant in your arms.

EVERYTHING REFERS TO SOMETHING, AND SOME THINGS TO EVERYTHING
(the Musings of Crashaw Pin)

*

This account of my years concerns attachment, detachment, disguise, renunciation. Have you been there too, Reader, in a way? Regarding devotion? The offering up of a life to reverence? No wonder I focused on Crashaw among the Metaphysicals, he with his utter passion for Church and Trinity.

EVERY MAN IS A GREAT MAN...IN DISGUISE!
(the musings of Crashaw Pin)

2.

To start at the start, I was conceived and nine months later midwifely delivered on a tourist boat slowly navigating the Nile. The Blue Nile, that is, where my parents, escapees eight years earlier from a queasy Vienna just after the *Anschluss*, served as long term entertainers and creatures-of-all-work on an old boat lumbering from one Egyptian spectacle to another. The first songs these ears likely heard were those of Kurt Weil, sung (you might say gargled) by my handsome ex-economist father. To this day I've chanted such pieces myself with an approach to the vibrato of a *Strassensanger*. However, Nile tourist business became cruelly unsettled during the Cold War's early 50's, so our little family relocated to the small town of Cranbury, New Jersey, immensely cute, a National Historic District, home to Hamilton, once headquarters for Washington, red brick inns and fabled schools, the whole bit. We settled at a distance from the center, at an egg farm on the flats a few miles out, where both parents, me too, worked under a sort of feudal lord, Mr. Mogul, egg business owner, whom I came — wrongly, it turns out — to despise. Through friends of friends he'd arranged the needed guarantee of our future financial stability — you couldn't get in without such sponsorship — and we labored to requite the favor.

Oh, those eggs! Brown and tiny, often double-yoked. My job from the age of three to hunt them out of the grass in what we now call free-range conditions. I learned my earliest Americanisms from Mr. Mogul, while my inheritance from my father Usher came down to a certain in-built flexibility, so I believe, plus an openness to challenge and a basic (if sometimes perverted) generosity of nature. My father was a kindly, patient man, though saddened and weary. He paid me a never-begrudged penny per found egg. He called me his noble *searching crew, die Durchsuchungcrew*. My parents were extremely generous with me. When I'd grown to the point where my woolen socks could no longer be pulled high enough to cinch with the blouse-ends of my old-worldy corduroy knickers — 'Ma," I'd cry, like the bleat of a baby goat, "I'll miss the bus. It's so *unfair!*" — they bought me, in Paterson, what we called then big boy pants. Such pleasure it was to get rid of those damned knickers that rasped all day with their zipping sound and marked me as a cursed outsider. At seven, there I was, wearing true pants that flowed right down to the shoe tops.

Helping out in our drafty share-cropper house where Father Usher and Mother Jen and I served twelve penny-pinching years, I gained not only a sharp eye for eggs but more importantly a sense of individual *difference*. There was my kind father, once a scholar, next a cabaret *hat-und-cane-mahn*, forever unable to profit from his Heidelberg doctorate, candling small brown eggs into the night, and my mother Jenny, gentle as a songbird, devoted not to her songbird profession but to motherhood, caretaker of the kitchen and the vegetable garden, and of me, her eventually self-named and *different* Crashaw.

3.

Different? This remains a question, for so much about humans, despite age, gender, nationality, seems the same.

ALL SO DIFFERENTLY THE SAME!
(Pin-musing)

Isn't this the case? Example: don't we all yearn for some kind of commitment? To an art, perhaps, or a family, maybe to a cause or to a fetching maiden in need of rescue. *Semper Fi.* My particular insight as to a lurch toward large yearnings, long in preparation, crystallized on a trip to Manhattan via the Staten Island Ferry in 1977, the water exceedingly cruel. Well, that's one story, the brutal image of Pin dunked away into ultimate darkness in the very year of his greatest worldly success. A more probable version depends on a "last seen" teaser tacked to the photo-wall of the "disappeared." This major happening occurred on a brilliant spring day, April 22nd to be exact, a Saturday (also, it happens, the very day Dr Allen Bussey completed, in that year alone, 20,302 yo-yo loops — you can discover just about anything via the internet — and yes, that reference gives something of my live-or-die timing away. We even have Wi-Fi (rather wobbly) where I've chosen, covertly, to reside. No, I didn't jump or get pushed from the ferry into permanent absence, though rumors flourished for a time. What did take place was a burst of insight, long on the way, that eventually led me to renounce the usual gobbling-ups of this earthly state. More about this shortly. I'd been reading dharma texts for years — "dharma," the way things are — at first for poetic inspiration, later because I was hooked. Yet meanwhile, until that historic Saturday on the ferry, I'd functioned in terms of a self-serving work-ethic which I called *The Morality of the Percussionist*, namely an all too familiar urgency to sweat non-stop for status and success.

When I chose instead to fade away like a wraith through the ferry-side fog at the Battery, I immediately suffered the usual losses of the Renunciate, loss of friends, of a fabled city, of a small but precious garden. Also: no more ballet, no Mozart in performance, no morning bagel-with-schmeer. Plus the abandonment of dear bedmates, this the deepest cut of all, since you can't both be there as a lover and disappear at exactly the same moment. Yet think of what I gained from an extremely early retirement through opportunities I came to label The *Devotion of the Percussionist*. If rhythm-section Morality involves an Iron Law against premature cessation — one *must* drum on — *Devotion* is a deeper matter.

Stay with me on this a moment — and please forgive that, as a quirky poet, I tend to drift into figurations echoing my Metaphysical namesake, poor short-lived Richard Crashaw (1613–1649).

Here's what I mean by distinguishing the Morality of action from Devotion to same. Every beat-keeper is obligated not to flag, for otherwise the musical structure totters. A drummer (sometimes instead a stand-up bass, or a lone guitar might serve, or in extreme cases an umpah tuba) a drummer must work while even piccolos rest. You might say a trustworthy percussionist, even before Devotion clicks in, is already a *Bodhisattva* of sorts, putting out for the grouply good. But a champion of ongoingness needs to reach further, give up credit and calculation, become a creature at one with ongoingness. They exclaim in Tibet "AH HO," AH meaning the-nature-of-things and HO the wondrous, delicious fact that earthly items have been provided to fill up the resplendence of Essence.

Take the image of scat-singing, a nearby cousin to drumming: those nonce syllables for which we go to school to Ella and

79

Louie, rapidly invented and meaningless sounds releasing a patter trippingly from the tongue in substitution for absent lyric. The production of such tipsy runs of verbal energy can be guided by will, no question, but scat-singing works best by not calculating the next *ratta-tata-plata-plax*, by letting random utterance occur in a sort of unconscious way. That's what I mean by *Devotion*, the trust that the source will provide, that outpour indeed will pour out. Otherwise we are doomed to act as if whatever happens comes from our own straining wit or will or demanding standards alone. Drummers know what I mean. Singers and Salesmen and Actors and Teachers, too. It's the same, by the way, with tabla *gats* as with Ella-scats. And of course the same with love-making. *Devotedly*, we proceed. No need to calculate, we simply accept the gift. This became one of the greatest of the rewards granted me, a release from the willful domination of a personal story-line into Big Story itself, transformed from tripping over my toes to flowing with the flows.

Some have called this the power of *Mu*.

QUESTION: IS MU A SOUND MADE BY A COW?
ANSWER: MU

Trusting that skat syllables will arrive without beckoning as you scoot your way drumming over the cliff of the moment marks the risk of faith allowing those fine rhythms of love or music or any-thing else to maintain themselves without anxiety. You don't have to create flow, flow *flows*, trust me. Oh, I tell you, this realization was so helpful after years of striving out of obligation and hunger for so-called "triumph," while ignorant of forces hidden from my self-obsessed eyes.

And you, Reader?

I note the shadows lurking in my own inner-nature, but am not given admission to your hiddenness, except through what you might choose to tell me. And much of that would be lies, no?

80

Admit it. Lies usually of omission, granted, for the sake of social acceptance, for the safety of respectability. Take, for example, sexual desire, which is often assumed to vary greatly in intensity along the human continuum. Yet who knows, for sure? All so differently the same. Your pert-prim-proper young lady, say, what's happening within those skirts, in that brain and bosom? And will she ever provide a report, for the good uses of science if for no other reason? Rarely. Well, and the males are liars too. Some even wear bowties. Once a woeful young lady I was lucky enough to have lying beside me partially unclothed on my narrow bed in my narrow student dorm room, spoke shyly of experiencing a "wide-on," a locution and condition that came to me as a revelation in that year of my Bachelor's degree. *Ahha,* I thought, *they* too can be roused to a telling point. Her condition (and mine) needless to say, was shortly, with groans and breathings, resolved.

This very first Pin conquest, if we wish to call it that, took place with Goldie Bush — an actual, substantial red-haired girl of that astounding name — about whom details will follow. She was a close friend of our crowd's favorite representative of the desired-opposition, the freshman female who earned the status of being one of the senior *guys*, an honorary boy, Stella Rhondo Beck (I use actual names with impunity, since no one beyond myself except for you, imagined Reader, will ever see these pages, and face it, you're *imaginary*).

Goldie Bush and Stella Rhondo Beck were escapees from Bowling Green, Kentucky, entering our northern Ivy League school in the year when we were readying to leave. Since kindergarten they'd been placed side by side on schedules and rosters, Beck and Bush. By college they'd already taken increasingly different paths as to their sexuality. Bush loved the sport, God bless her, and her buddy Beck tended to provide occasions. Our beloved Beck could have been one of those helper-ladies in porn flicks who stand around urging the main fuckee to get on with it, holding her hair out of the camera's view.

81

Goldie actually frightened me with her undaunted voracity. She was a noisy reactor, starting with the merest nipple-touch, and at culmination, wow, verbal fireworks. There's nothing better than a loved one's satisfaction-sound, but Goldie was in all ways extreme. It took connivance on SRB's part, getting me drunk at a party at a local friend's parent-emptied house to hook me up with Goldie that first time, and then Goldie wanted to go for three sessions at various awakenings through the night. Another joining came a while later when she entered my dorm room without knocking. "Just wanted to see what you were doing before you hide the evidence." She claimed, quite simply, to be a sex addict, ideally needing a carnal wrestle about twice a day. "You have no idea," she said, "how exhausting it is for a girl to find herself a little cock in this Victorian town."

"Does it have to be little?"

My college friends and I felt blessed to have attracted the attentions of the pair Bush & Beck. I believe others among the five of us had at least one sweaty experience with Goldie, and we all loved the unobtainable Beck, aspiring to cohabit with that long thin body of hers, crazed, even, o woe, by her claiming an iron-clad, chastity-belt-level commitment to maintaining her virginity. We at times would call her by her initials "SRB," in the style of a corporate executive.

"Got a wood-event in the crotch here, SRB, oh what to do?"

"Enjoy, Baby. You've also inherited a sturdy prehensile hand, no shame to it, or so I've heard. But you know, I'm the Virgin Queen."

"You're the Virgin-*Mean*, SB. C'mon. Help out this sinkable ship. Uh-oh, gosh, we're passing beyond wood, this here's a case of steel upping toward titanium."

Did she ever give in? Certainly not while we were still undergrads in the year of our Lord 1969, all of us hanging out together. But later? We heard she'd gone at last for women; my friend Nils passed this info on when by chance he ran into her several years later after she'd finished med school and taken up the practice of pediatrics in Santa Fe. If you happen to be a woman and your lovers also happen to be women, do you remain a virgin — in some technical sense — forever? I had to ask, jerk that I was, even characterizing the question as one that might bring a man trembling before a feminist tribunal and its firing squad at dawn without even the solace of a pre-cigarette. Yes, when I visited SRB in New Mexico following Nil's investigative reporting, I actually asked about — among other things — just that, the state of her famous chastity. As a kind of joke, of course. And she did laugh. "Ah, Benji, " she said — my birth-name before the heteronym "Crashaw" came into play — "dear intractable Benj, *you're* the lifelong virgin!"

WOMEN ARE ALSO *PEOPLE* — IMAGINE!

4.

Before she found her feet in lesbian territory, what was it like for SBR to play a part among our horny crowd of guys, young bodies and libidos she had no carnal taste for? So male and basketball-tall she was, for all her fine beauty, that in our wanderings through downtown Philadelphia she'd be the first as a matter of course to mount a steel fence standing in our exploratory way, helping us, her mates, to ease down from the top on the other side. A sweet, playful person. I thought she actually liked me more than a little back then, but learned otherwise. She still kept her almost whitish hair spiky short on top in Santa Fe as she had those years before when she wore sleeveless undershirts in warm weather that revealed her nipples to a killing degree.

When we reconnected in relative maturity that weekend in '75 we wandered the Santa Fe galleries, took in a performance of *Turandot*, ate stupendously, and talked — the chat not just looking back on student days but dealing with more or less everything. "We're so much alike," I told her, "it should follow that we'd already be married with two and a half kids and a kidney-shaped swimming pool, all helped along thanks to my inheritance from superbly frugal Usher and Jen."

"Yeah. Somebody up there sure has a wicked sense of humor."

A PERFECT MATE HANGS HER PICTURE IN HER PARTNER'S MIRROR

5.

I met Stella's partner Denise only toward the end of my weekend visit. She'd been off gigging with her band, *The Stark-Blind Ladies*. We settled at what they called their "haunt," not a bar but a Japanese restaurant with a line of tiny round outdoor tables just off the cobbled walkway, Nippon beer umbrellas, silk peonies in fake crystal squat vases. I ordered a large Saki for the three of us and Denise knocked down her little white cupful in Japanese style as if it were a shot glass. I could tell I made her nervous. We'd exchanged no more than the usual pleasantries while being introduced. From SRB's furtive smile I could see she was proud of her Denise, a buff woman improbably even an inch taller than Stella, one who in a more recent day we would have called "hot." Most striking about her was her great cascade of auburn hair and her especially large eyes, — hydrocephalic? — eyes with a suspicion of green to them. Does *freckled* make any sense in describing eyes? A few tiniest dots appeared toward the limbus, attractive somehow. Denise as a person seemed austere until something funny came along and then that bray of her laugh was startling.

"So," I asked, "you guys been together long?"

"Four months, twelve days, seventeen hours," said Stella

Rondo.

"Uh, *serious*. 'Let me count the days'."

"Why are you here?" asked Denise suddenly, flatly.

Well. How do you respond to an aggression like that? I never knew what to make of the sudden hostility of this Denise. Jealousy? Seems improbable. In defense I shrugged my shoulders, I panned my comic's hands, I turned to Stella for help, but she stared at something in outer space.

I chose to answer the attack with a question of my own. "And you, Denise?"

"I'm here for the flamingo roll. And also to try to figure you out, Mr. Benji."

"Any progress?"

"I've ordered the flamingo roll. You, on the other hand, remain...opaque."

"Dennie," said Stella Rondo, "please. Manners!"

"Oh that," said her friend.

The waiter, Caucasian, hovered in an "everything all right?" sort of way, but also nearly crouching like a prey animal coming alert to danger and veering off elsewhere, sensing the heat at our tiny table.

This was a year before my first book appeared, two years before it amazingly copped the Pulitzer.

But my report of a killer Santa Fe moment may prove misleading, for there'd been more cheerful chat between me and Stella before no-nonsense Denise appeared and moved in for the kill.

"Denise doesn't mean to be cruel, Benji, she's just heard a lot of nostalgic stuff about me and the boys before you all graduated, what with the teasing and like that going on. She's just protective, is all."

"Stop being so fucking *nice*, Stell'! The guy turns up as an old friend who never stopped trying to get into your pants and making you the butt of all sorts of abusive gender shit because he's so fuckin' clever and you feeling you have to treat him as something

85

other than what he is, namely a joke, right, like all your other so-called buddy-boys! *Manners*? With the sexist pig he so shiningly is?"

"Jesus," said Stella, placing a hand not on her but on my shoulder, "calm down!" I signaled for the check. The water asked if everything had been okay and I barked a laugh. And then they wouldn't even let me handle the bill. Talk about methods of domination! We wound up splitting three ways, three different credit cards. I exited the situation with lots to think about, but not really feeling majorly hurt. What had I expected, after all? That SRB would want to treat my visit as a chance for slipping back into undergraduate cuteness and adventure as when we used to sneak her into the men's quad ducking her under the guards' window wearing a hat to conceal her stray ringlets?

Had we taken advantage of poor Stella back at school? It was she who'd cultivated us, after all. It wasn't more than a week after she'd reached Philly that she'd picked up a part-time job at Manic Mary's, the drugstore cum soda fountain directly across the trolley tracks from the male dorms. I don't think there'd ever been an actual Manic Mary, only a name, a cuteness for the delectation of the cuteness-loving undergraduates of our day. There were usually five of us, close companions, all male, who treated the place as a clubhouse, usually able to settle in at the one large sprawling booth at the back. For some unknown reason we liked to cause little fires as we talked and debated and bragged and joked and craned our necks to check out the girls at the fountain sipping their cherry cokes. The fires, fueled by napkins and drinking straw wrappers, would drive the manager crazy, which of course was the point. They really weren't dangerous fires, nicely contained in our tall iced cream soda glasses with the fluted edges. But there's satisfaction to be gained from girl-shrieks of disaster-discovery and the manager rushing over schloshing a pitcher of water which she didn't mind wetting us with as she doused one or another conflagration.

86

"Damn you boys," she'd cry. "I shouldn't let you in the door. You swore you wouldn't do this any more."

"Never trust the oath of a poet," Nic told her, my closest buddy and roommate, "poets burn not with a small but a large gem-like flame. However, they keep it in an iced-cream soda glass, for safety's sake." Nic was working at his beard at the time, hoping for a largish bush in homage to his idol Thelonius Monk, spinning around the way Monk did, walking away then coming back with an incomprehensible mumble like the great piano-banger himself.

How we loved simply saying things and doing improbable things! In those days any one of us might have been capable of writing a Marx Brothers movie. Arlo, who wound up as an architect in Ann Arbor, well, I hope he hasn't arranged for any built-in weaknesses that eventually would bring a building down. We did have some restraint; the anarchy was mainly verbal.

About the soda-glass fires, Nic would say "You know you'd miss us, Charleen, if you put us on your shit-list." This was an invention of George ("the Guk"), always calling the poor manager lady "Charleen," the devil knows why, since her red name-tag gleamed right there: Lucile.

SRB came over to the booth in her little apron and cleaned up the mess, wagging an index finger at us like a loving big sister. I wrote that year — the year of Bush & Beck — one of my earliest little teaser pieces just to use the name Charleen, for the sake of the winsome lilt of the name itself, managing to get it in twice, in fact. When this poem of mine was miraculously published in an infinitely Little magazine later that year, Lucile the manager seemed honestly touched when I gave her my copy. The poem ended, after playing around quite a bit near-nonsensically in my manner at the time:

Uh-oh, there goes that poet Crashaw Pin,
he's a-teeter, a twitter, a tottler risking

the topmost rung of his flimsy ladder,
please have a care there, Crash, don't crash.

Charleen, when you and I started this poem
did you give a thought, intense Charleen,
to the chance that it might reach its ending so badly?
But there you go, rushing in as you do,
reading my moon-drenched, mismatched-stuff!

POETS ARE PIGS FOR ENDORPHANS, JUST LIKE EVERYBODY ELSE, ONLY WEARING HIGH-HEELS AND DANCING BACKWARDS

6.

What is it about artsy young folks and their impassioned silliness? We sobered up, of course, once Chicago in '68 brought the long delayed news to our conservative campus that something rather huge was underway in the world out there, centered on Viet Nam — matters worthy of brave protest. We became at least mildly politicized, doing marches if not sit-ins or bombings. Then my buddies to a man went on to various graduate schools, no matter their zest for demonstrating against the war, while I, in dread of the effect on the tongue and soul of toxic academic language, joined the army instead. Don't ask if I ever killed anyone during my two year stint, give me a break. They kept me stateside, teaching military law and functional psychology to prospective MPs at Fort Dix. I even visited my doddering parents in Cranberry on several weekends to help chicken-farm, such a blessing, for how could I know that they would both check out a few years later, foxing their dual diagnosis of Non-Hodgkin's lymphoma and leaving me a surprisingly substantial bundle. Jennie departed by means of a plastic bag over the head plus multiple pills, while

Usher at the same time flashed out by means of a small pistol we never knew he owned. I mourned them, of course, for the sweet people they were, so incredibly good to me. That's another story, painful to tell. For years I had to remind myself — just about every third hour — that there wouldn't have been anything I could have done for them as they failed in capacity toward the end and decided not to stretch the misery out. They never even told me they were ill.

Meanwhile, I loved the army. In fact, as my poem-publishing and consequent teaching gigs took over afterwards, I sometimes wondered if I shouldn't have followed a military career and saved the world from many brain-twinging stanzas and lines. The appeal of military service? Exactly what's often said: brotherhood. This whole world-system seemed to me then to insist in terms of a massive urge toward individual notoriety, no matter what my Buddhist books advised, while far from needing to stand out from the pack what we really needed was the pack itself. To belong, to exist more modestly as a vital part of something, rather than to vaunt one's special distinction and wind up feeling like a loner.

Speaking of packs, before passing on from college days I should add a bit more about our style as undergraduates, since something similar characterizes my Crashaw-work, a certain resistance to the enticements of maturity. Back then we had a taste, as I've said, for invention for its own sake, nonstop, everything anarchic and spontaneous, acts and jokes always intending a tang of daring. Well, the best explanation for this is that the zest for play can extend far beyond late adolescence, a transmogrification of love for the exploratory pleasures of childhood. We literally could not get enough of low-level anarchy. Example: Stella, even sometimes Bush, would now and then stay overnight at our dorm, too late to stumble all the way across campus to their officially allotted female beds. SRB bunked in on such occasions on a pallet that

Eddie kept for her in his room. She slept there because Eddie became born-again back in high school and so had principles to cultivate and never would make a play for her the way Guk and Nik and Aldo and I did. Since Ed displayed a prominent adam's apple and was prematurely bald, our small-statured, small featured buddy simply assumed no female would ever take an interest in him. We argued the point, tried to set him up, played amateur psychiatrists with poor gentle Ed, but to no avail. He, of course, had the best fun-friendship of us all with SRB, uncomplicated by our vaunted rage of hormones.

Well, one Saturday she and he rose early, took themselves over to the diner on Chestnut Street for a pancake breakfast, and returning found that The Guk down the hall, at about ten a.m., was still abed. This inspired them to hunt up some rope down in the janitor's basement, sneak in covertly and draw the coil of rope clenching round after round under the bed frame and across the shoulders, tight around waist, ankles, impulsively attaching poor George to his cot. SRB and I talked about this stunt among others during my visit to Santa Fe. "Stupid stupid stupid, why did we do stuff like that," she exclaimed. "So cruel! Thinking it was a mark of genius or something." She shook her head from side to side as if to toss the memory away. What had happened — and we all got into it — was that George, tied to his cot as a kind of an equivalent for the stocks in Puritan days — in this case for being a slugabed — was paraded out to a display in the main quad where we approximated his bedroom (I carried his stand-up reading lamp; Aldo lugged his mirror). We took photos. The Guk nobly kept his silence throughout the ordeal. We wheeled him round to the nursing school and serenaded the nurses a while and then we left him propped upright against a tree, narrow bed and all, in the Arboretum, where his philosophy TA found him hours later and released him while famously remarking, "Mr. Troutlein, you've chosen a fetching way to protest against Heideggerian angst."

BAD EGGS DRIVE OUT GOOD…
ISN'T THAT THE REAL GRESHAM'S LAW?

Yet even now I'm still not coming clean with you, Reader, so difficult is it to face the truth if the whole story be told. My consciously jaunty tone in what I've written so far has served as an act of commission veiling darker acts of omission. For in Santa Fe that time, SRB and I at last spoke at some length concerning the fate of poor, driven Goldie Bush. Goldie, who would say, ganja-high, "oh, bore, bore!" of our so-called intellectual chatter, and then, once more, with what can only be described as a killer smile, "can't we just get naked and be happy?" A tad over-weight from falling back on chocolate when body joys ran sparse, funny and brash and loveable in her way, but a sort of an overwhelming presence.

"What was going on with you two that year? You urged her along?"

"I'm still trying to work that out," Stella told me. "I guess I'd been in love with her from an early age, 'cause I couldn't help but admire the way she played her sort-of slut-hood against my timidity, it was like we sort of conducted a long conversation between two best-friends, some kind of pride-thing there for both of us. But where is she now? We lose touch with everyone."

"What else, Stell'? I can see in your face you have something more to tell me."

You'll understand at this point, Reader, why we've heard so little about Goldie from me. Evasion. Man-up, Benji. Tell — or at least let SRB speak it out.

"She was three months pregnant with your baby when you left for the army."

Do I need to note how these words from SRB brought me to an absolute halt?

91

"The sex on that scene," she said.

" — <u>ob</u>-scene," I threw in. "Jesus, Stell', pregnant with my baby? How do you know? How could anybody really know such things back then?"

Such was my immediate self-defensive turn.

"That's what Goldie said. She had the dates all charted out. You were the last unprotected prick inside her."

"Jesus. Did she *have* the kid?"

Stella shrugged, maybe feigning ignorance. "Wish I could say. I feel really awful about the whole thing. I encouraged her to experiment while faking my own status with that chastity-belt business."

"Your virginity-claim was a lie?"

"Ah, Benji, there *are* no nineteen-year-old virgins in Bowling Green, Kentucky! How naive can you get? No, that Virgin Queen bit was my undergraduate contraception device. Self protection has always been my M.O., the tom-boy stuff itself was just a version of that. I liked being funny with the boy-crowd, I liked passing as one of you guys. Can you imagine what my life would have been like those days if I'd slept with any of you?"

"But you were already tending...?"

"I always suspected it would ultimately be women for me. Yet when I think about it, why did Beck and Bush turn into such a teaser of a tag-team? And why won't Goldie make contact with me any more? I write her all the time, care of her mother, but the letters come back from Kentucky marked *Return to Sender*."

"You'd slept with girls already, with women, back then?"

"Yeah. I'd been with women. Just like you, you unregenerate prick!"

COULD IT BE THAT FOLKS DISLIKE THEMSELVES FOR PERFECTLY GOOD REASONS?

7.

To keep the timing straight, let me point out that I'd had carnal congress with Goldie Bush on exactly two different occasions and no more. We were wild that first night, less the follow-up later, and to tell the truth she frightened me with her excess of feeling. I had to cut the connection off. She looked elsewhere for a partner...partners. But I didn't leap to contradict her sense — as confided to SRB — that I was the father of her child...assuming she'd actually birthed and kept that child, our child, but what was I supposed to *do*? And where was she hanging out? She'd disappeared, at least from the knowledge of her school friends like SRB. Reader, I think you'll expect that my next step would be to set out manfully to find and save Goldie, but that's Television. I could have started by trying to contact her through a friend of mine in Lexington, but no, I was scared out of my mind, for searching might actually turn Goldie up and then what? Was I to devote the rest of my still young and aspiring life to supporting nymphomaniacal Goldie Bush plus her consequent offspring? The notion put me in mind of the suicidal inseminating flights of drone bees, of the Queen-tending sacrifices of courtier ants.

A not very heartening attitude, I'll admit. Books advising writers usually point out that there's nothing like a sympathetic protagonist to lift a piece, nudge it toward appeal from the get-go. So surely I'm a shameful disappointment and I'm pained by it. No question, at this point in my adventures I was, as SRB's Denise exactingly pointed out, something of a joke.

I did worry about Goldie, and I brooded over what had led her through those college days to spend herself as she did, in a sort of desperation. I came to believe she only felt real when touched, rushed, tongued, penetrated — by giving over, is that it? Is that what they feel? When I knew her so briefly — in the Biblical sense — no such questions came alive for me, each of the three couplings that first time a true pleasure. I recall her unsheathing her bra, maybe a cue there, for it was a formidable garment, a sort of harness for ponderous breasts. She had a mother-being in her, a Crashaw-like "feminine" sensibility. Richard Crashaw was constantly partial to maternal imagery in his verse, T. S. Eliot among the first to appreciate that there was also "brainwork" behind the seeming perversity and outrageousness of Crashaw's overwrought language. Goldie, I concluded was the careless protector of near-infinite eggs. I see her in memory beneath me as I plunged and sped, her eyes tight as if in pain, as if she were giving birth, achieving. Something she said after our first love-making together has stayed with me for a lifetime. This was during aftertime, cigarette and chatting time. She kissed my shoulder. I sighed with ease. She half-whispered: "I still can feel you inside me."

She was too much for me, too powerfully driven, too emotional, too needy. I just had to break it off.

8.

I think this is the moment to go into what happened to me on that famous Staten Island ferry in my twenty-eighth year, sailing from St. George Terminal to Whitehall Terminal. I experienced there a sort of half-hour entrance into a private philosophical graduate school, a confirmation of studies I'd undertaken on my own quite a while before. What Guru Yang saw in me that led to his intervention will remain forever a mystery. Let's call it an impulse toward grace or simply an instinct of need (are those one and the same?) My Goldie-fears were much with me at that time. I imagined she might turn up to make demands for marriage and child-raising as a sort of death-in-life. I wouldn't go searching for her but I assumed she could find me whenever she wanted to, and such paranoid musings misted my thinking with repeated anxiety. DNA testing for paternity was still in its infancy then, far from a little cheek squab or hair sample now, but I'd heard about

94

it as a coming technology that might resolve the question as to who at least was clearly *not* the putative Dad.

Did the good Guru pick up on my unpleasant inner state, as if by scent?

"Beautiful, no?" he said. We stood on the forward deck as the Ferry welcomed its final autos from Staten Island and prepared for the journey. Far ahead, still in the miniaturized distance, the Great City lay in toy-like scale, almost comically unimposing though ultimately all-consuming as we travelers became in turn ant-like, immersed as the buildings grew overwhelmingly tall above us.

Guru Yang. What can I tell you about him? We only knew each other for one half hour. He was this curious-looking Indian man with ravaged teeth wearing a flasher's khaki raincoat despite the considerable warmth of the weather as he spoke to me in the way one chats with a stranger in a public place. And all the while throwing now and then bread bits toward the ferry-accompanying gulls.

LET *BUDDHA U.* BUDDHA-YOU

"I see you are troubled," was what the Guru offered for starters. "Yes, I read minds. I imagine I should ask permission, I'm sure this is invasive, but I fail to act properly about such matters, having become by now a shameless New Yorker."

"And before...?

"Only a shameless vibrating mote in the Universe. Like all the rest. An eel-like vibrating congeries of strings. A sort of Rabbi, if you will, in the long line from the great Jewish poet Jesus."

So this, I thought, would be that sort of conversation.

"Let me buy you a topped-up swirl of chocolate iced cream over there," said my self-appointed consultant, "anything to cheer you up. My God, young man! What have you done? Have you killed someone?"

95

"Not that I know of. Wouldn't your psychic talent give you the answer to such a question?"

"No. Pervasive misery I see but not its source. I also am aware of your clever dodging that serves to veil the truth of things from others and yourself. What is your name, young buffer, if I may ask?"

And right there I faced a quandary. I didn't give him Benji. I gave him Crash.

WE ALL SPLASH ABOUT IN OUR OWN SALT POOLS OF TEARS

The concluding lines of one of my undergraduate poems has just this minute returned to mind as I sit writing in the greenery-shrouded sunshine of my back yard on my yellow-lined pad, words later to be polished as they go into my laptop. The poem, or at least its ending, yearns to be included at this point. It touches on Goldie inevitably, the sense I was left with that I'd taken advantage of her, treated her like some sick animal vulnerable to predation. The build of the piece concerns a sadistic hero-cop on a motorcycle who runs down a speeding blonde in a convertible (I'd actually witnessed just such a scene, driving properly at the highway speed limit myself). The cop gazes down at this blonde, begins to write her a ticket while "wearing a cheetah's grin."

The poem ends:

> you pass him leaning toward his kill...
> you who have feasted on slow-moving strays,
> on starvelings lost at the edge of the herd.

But who is this "you," Mask'-Man? Come on!

Well, the whole *megilla* is called shame, using the troubled as if they were prey. Shameful Male Lust. My namesake had considerably much to say on this and related subjects.

Peace, good reader, do not weep;
Peace, the lovers are asleep.

— Richard Crashaw

9.

The fact that I didn't undertake a search for Goldie, as a Hollywood hero would have, stayed much with me. I never for long stopped thinking about her and our possible offspring, days and nights for years and years. At this very moment, too, of course. You know how a thought, some hurt or unfairness, will live with you like an unwanted guest and never go home? A permanent guest who hates you, surely, dedicated to making you suffer and miss the pure enjoyment of living. I thought of Goldie and Maybe-Little-Goldie not so much with concern and compassion as with fear and self-contempt.

The insane advent of my Pulitzer book only made my inner weather more gloomy. I re-read Dostoyevsky to make the worst even more worse, killing the old pawnbroker lady in imagination and feeling the impulse to confess with my gorge rising.

The Pulitzer came as an amazement. It was my first book, after all, no one on the jury of Big Shots could ever have heard of me, many of the poems were incomprehensibly playful, all four of my competitor poets were tenured "names." How it happened we'll never know, but there are theories, namely that the judges — even greater Big Shots than my competition — generated a rather nasty glee by passing over four 90-caliber word-warriors in favor of a small university press's pistol of a near-unknown. Once the announcement was made the deluge commenced. I was actually asked for autographs on the street! I had photographers and interviewers crowding me up to my dazzled eyes. The poetry prize always comes at the very end of Pulitzer news in the papers, accounts starting with the journalism categories as a matter of course, poetry limping in at the finish line.

THERE HAS NEVER BEEN A LEVEL PLAYING FIELD

But Guru Yang — where did *his* improbable advent come from, his name like mine an oddity?

"A name especially chosen just for you, Mister Crashaw. Are you sure I am not here solely as a product of your metaphysical imagination?"

He'd even heard of my 17th century forebear, which places him, I'd guess, in about the zero-zero-point-one percent of the literate population. When the actual Crashaw wrote: "What mine own madnesses have done with me," he had in mind his sin and abasement before God, a God who mysteriously choose to concern Himself with such a worm.

I could see his point.

"Oh yes, Crashaw," noted the Guru. "If we had no Donne, we'd always have Crashaw to fall back on."

"You know your Crashaw?"

"Who doesn't?"

"Everybody."

Then the man astounded me by commencing briefly to recite. A word or so might have strayed away from the 17th century original but why sweat the details? He quoted two appropriate lines from Crashaw's adaptation of Psalm 23: "simple weaknesse strayes, / (Tangled in forbidden wayes)." And I was stunned. Turned out he'd taken an English First at Cambridge, Pembroke College, Crash's college before that pious youth moved on to even more Catholic Peterhouse down the street. Pembroke College — Pembroke Hall back then — had connections with the poet Spencer, too, a more familiar figure who supposedly planted the very oak still happily flourishing in the Pembroke yard. The poem from Crash the Guru recited was, granted, one of his tiny epigrams, yet even so! To hear it from a stranger on the Staten Island Ferry!

> Silence, and sacred rest; peace, and pure joys;
> Kind loves keep house, lie close, and make no noise.

11.

The Guru and I went inside to the broad seating area — too much spray at the prow for comfort — and he explained his "community services." He had decided that taking fees was corrupting to the soul, but that a man must eat, so he divided his time into segments, rode the ferry every other weekday to his office on Fulton Street where paying clients arrived, and on Tuesdays and Thursdays served random sufferers he encountered during his day-long series of back and forth ferry-rides. His home and family nested on the Island. His wife worked as a free-lance editor for business publications. I'd been added, just like that, to his charity file, the sort of thing that was always happening to me.

People have always given me gifts. What can I do? Please don't hate me for it. Consider, for example, how our little family escaped obliteration at the hands of the devil Hitler, and just in the nick. And, granted that Mr. Mogul of Cranbury gave Child-Me a hard time — "you pee once more against tree, little Nazi, I cut from you your silly pecker!" — mostly my days had been pure gold. I read in English from the age of three, school prizes again and again settled upon my little laurel'd head, meanwhile I was doted upon by girls and later even by women. It seems strange, unaccountable, that a person so well-treated by the world and so enamored of its riches should become the defended recluse I am now. Fact is, after that first overly rewarded book of mine I never worked at bringing together another. Could be only Guru Yang would fully understand the dynamic involved in such a decision, the urge to stop living for a profit, to simply enjoy being alive and useful instead.

"A POET LOOKS AT THE WORLD
THE WAY A MAN LOOKS AT A WOMAN"
— *Wallace Stevens*

"What brings you to the Island?" the Guru enquired during our ferry consultation.

"Visiting a friend. Tomorrow I have to bare my soul on morning TV."

"Ah, I sensed an anticipatory anxiety. The good-morning-to-you kind of show? — sickeningly warm-hearted? Yes, I've paused over those, the people there are so, how do you say, chipper? Most unreal."

"This experience of the Pulitzer prize has been beyond-unreal."

"You've done something newsworthy. I understand. The public is then obliged to bleed you to death."

"Yes. The gods have outrageously blessed me so now life must turn into an unceasing PR tour."

"I do realize. I've seen this face of yours a while ago in print, which drew my attention today. From a *Times* front section, in fact. You have won a distinction. Should I offer congratulations? By the way, is this your true name, *Crashaw*? Are you sure?"

"What they call a heteronym, a pen-name, you know?"

"Your own name, your real name, is, so to speak...?"

"Just call me Crash."

"Well, Crash, I am here to serve you. Tell. Tell me your problem."

"I can have only one?"

"Touché. But what we're involved with here is a limited-time party."

"And *your* name, Sir? Surely it's not —?"

The Guru confessed that he wasn't literally called Yang. "I

adjust the name and credentials to the needs of my clients."

"So I'm a client?"

"Sonny, your entire life is on the line."

"So what are your other names, Guru Yang? They say there's power in names."

"Yes, true. But in this case you don't want to know the whole startling list."

"Give me one, then."

"God. Used in extreme cases where one might say what's needed is the fear of God."

"Another. Give me another. Another magical name, my Guru."

"Crashaw Pin."

"Come on!"

He shrugged, flashed a toothy smile. "We have what? Roughly seventeen minutes? We must jump to the gist."

"Gladly," I agreed, and from that moment the playfulness was gone.

"You have much too low of an opinion of yourself, young man. You confuse your Crash-self with acts committed or not. Of a certainty you have been blessed, yet you miss enjoyment of such blessings, why is that?"

"My lost parents? The Holocaust? Bad karma?"

"All of the above?"

12.

Concerning my Problem, it took a signifying turn the following Monday as of my contracted jollification at Good Morning, America. The mystery of my doings and undoings should be clarifying a bit by now, dear Imaginary Reader. I am one of those who hope not to be blamed for the ugly stuff. Sartre has a compelling notion in this regard that I once appropriated to inhabit a poem.

STONEWORKERS

Sartre writes that all souls cry out
if you beat your soul...but you must go public.
Gag the poor thing in its feted cell
and you're comfortless, humming your dirge
"Why me? Why me the self-assassin?"

Tell us then how you seemed to be chosen
to slam your mind from wall to wall
while stoneworkers swagger home each night
(or so you think) for drink and sex
crying "Damn, but today we laid us some stone!"

A further confession — I came out with it to the Guru — was that I felt my nom de plume might provide a bit of protection against an inquiring Goldie. In this human jungle the prey animals get chased, but there are consequences. Was I supposed to seek her out, devote to her? Terrified, I didn't like this Benji guy who was terrified, who very much didn't like the idea that he might actually find her, with the kid, and by doing so commit a sort of social suicide. Not that hiding from Goldie's possible claims was the only determining factor in what I turned to next. No, I eased my way into nominal non-existence mainly because of what some might even label an enlightenment experience at the very brink of Gotham City. I'd written my forty-seven poems, painstakingly herded them into a book that Aldo's father — an English Professor at Tufts with connections — liked so well as to lead him to go out of his way to submit to a guy he knew at Oklahoma State University Press, and whoops, there they swooped into the Accepted File, were shepherded through the publishing process and, on a whim, someone sent four copies to the Pulitzer committee. Viola, the rest, you might say, became history, or better call it misery. The folks at OSUP were amazed and dazed, much more even than I, at having a Pulitzerized title on hand. And then came my ferry talk with Guru Yang adding to my own years of studying books of archaic teachings, all leading to my notorious turn away from notoriety into a sort of terminal silence.

13.

GURU YANG
Have you done some therapy, Poet? Seen
someone, as they say?

CRASH
That's what this is, ferry-theri-py?

YANG
Ah, phrase-maker. This cleverness of yours,
do you ever suspect it's a diabolical scheme
to forbid you from experiencing true feelings?

ME
Not except just about all the time.

YANG
Have you ever considered trying to become
just a normal human being? You know the
sort I mean? The sort uncompelled to tap-dance
down the sidewalk for applause? Have you
ever heard of The Great Middle Way?

ME
Gosh, Guru, you do rush along toward the
meat and potatoes!

But of course he would, this being what you might call speed-healing, to pirate a more recent term. We had about fifteen minutes left on the water before the city would take us over. A rather cloudy day for July, one of those glum days where poets, the Chosen People, tend to stay indoors smoking cigarettes, looking for a strong final line while crunching too many potato chips.

"I want you to pause," said Guru Yang with a sudden deepening of tone that announced a special seriousness. "We have all the time the schedule allows. I propose we meditate together and channel each other. Are you willing to do that? We dock at 4:17. It is now, let me see, 4:04. Thirteen minutes. No problem. We will sit in stillness in good posture and allow thoughts to come and go for, oh, ten of those thirteen minutes, accepting the conditions of Time, and then we will enjoy the rich offering of three minutes left to sum it all up and launch the next fifty or sixty years of your life, Mister Crashaw Pin. While we meditate, please understand, I expect you to think only my thoughts as I will think only yours — understood?"

We meditated, settling in misted chairs back out on the forward deck again, the city enlarging by the instant as we sailed closer. The ferry gave a hoot. We both laughed. I felt absolutely wonderful.

14.

Filled with thoughts of renunciation as stirred up by Guru Yang (his thoughts are the source, by the way, of my Gandhi slogan appearing below) I found my way to Pennsylvania Station and stood in the great rotunda there which Thomas Wolfe described as containing Time. Where to? Which way? As I stood so indecisively I was approached by a tall, beautiful black woman who said "You lookin' for a girl!" A declaration, not a question. Turns out she'd seen me glance questioningly down street after street as

104

I approached the station and thought, naturally, given the nature of the neighborhood that I was seeking paid connubiality. When I disappointed her — not without regret — confirming that I wasn't "lookin' for pussy" as she'd put it, "I run three blocks after you,' she said, "gimme sumpin'." And I did, I gave her a five (those were different days, monetarily speaking) and she wandered off elsewhere at her job of self-vending.

"You lookin' for a girl!" Prophetic words.

...PONDER GONE PASSIONS, DEVOTIONS, GRIEFS...
most of one line of a long poem by Crashaw Pin

15.

So, after all of that, sleepless, wracked, I simply blew off my appearance on the Monday morning talk show. I failed to warn, or announce, or turn up, I simply went underground. Shouldn't have done it that way, I know, leaving them with a two minute segment to fill on the fly (heavy on sniffy chat about my bad manners, I learned later). And of course — so stupid! — the attention my non-appearance elicited, the anger on TV turning into theories and concerns and the investigation consequently stirred up, made for a superplus of the very publicity I sought to avoid. The attention of the world for a time turned to trying to locate me as a missing person!

Here's the poem they'd expected me to read on the morning show as part of that failed guest appearance. I'd been asked to let them vet the poem in advance. They required a very short one. My choice wasn't written for the occasion, though I'd planned to fake that it was. I didn't blame them for checking it out, given the length and scandalous nature of some of the more carelessly playful pieces in EVEN HURRY SLOWLY, my improbable prize winner.

105

OM

There's a wind that clears the mind,
blows away mind's little winds,
invisablizing faces, places,
questioning all our stuff
down to paperclips and dust motes,
our entire story cleared away
leaving there a blessed sort of vacancy.
Wait. The movie will begin again, of course,
but briefly you exist as one long OM.

I'd planned to give them a Tuva-like deep-throat rendition of that last two-lettered mantra-word. I am capable of a deep sounding of OM. Yes, that primal syllable had thus a brief chance of resounding on American television, yet there I went, finking out on such an opportunity.

"RENOUNCE AND ENJOY"
                                        — *Gandhi*

16.

I think there are many versions of hell. Like the process of getting what you thought you'd wanted turning out to be exactly *not* what you wanted and having this event repeat eternally.

My own hell-version, at this break-away moment, turned out to be *Being Noted*, my name in the papers. I took a train to Portland, then a rental car up toward Bangor, just looking around, thinking Maine, under-populated, would suit a hermit poet. Down toward the coast in a rental car to Ellsworth I spent two wonderfully quiet days at Acacia National Park, and there I first heard about the five Cranbury islands, the one catching my attention, of course, being Little Cranbury. Yes, Little Cranbury Island, tempting for the irony of its name echoing the locus of my childhood, the larger Cranbury inappropriate for my long-arriving modesty of orientation. I stayed a week at the one bed & breakfast on the island, visited a few of the realtors in Great Cranbury's town of Isleton, and had the friend I hired to pick up my mail at the P.O. back in Manhattan send it north. I was just about to plunk a down-payment out of my stash — thanks to my self-deceased parents — to buy a small picturesque beachfront on Little Cranbury when irony came sashaying around again for its bow, preventing this sudden purchase which would have established me as perhaps the best fixed of about 150 residents on that tiny island. For when I had recently arrived letters read to me over the phone from NYC, mostly from people first congratulating me on the prize and next requesting that I transform them by magic into the company of the rich and famous, I received news about that other Cranbury, the New Jersey Cranbury. This letter was from a law firm. I had inherited a chicken farm and an egg business three miles from town from Mr. Mogul, who'd doted on me all along. There were words to that effect in his will. Plus a surprising outflow of guilt at his not being there for my deeply stricken Mom and Pop.

From one Cranbury to another. Such things happen; you don't even have to be in a Dickens novel. So I've resided since, unknowably, here in the Garden State, not that far from NYC itself, hiding away behind the chicken feathers, volunteering under an assumed name — you don't need to know that name, but it's not Bush — volunteering at the local hospice, still loyal to the practice Guru Yang in a few minutes established for me.

17.

"Okay," said the Guru out on the deck, removing a pair of ting-shas from his leather bag and creating three fierce ringings to begin our meditation, "Breathe."

I took, as instructed, three long breaths, and on the long release of the third and the start of breath number four the mental-movie wildly changed. Running through my consciousness no longer were the usual Pin thoughts regarding lust and regret and ambition and desire and lust plus lust. Now I had gone amazingly elsewhere, channeling Guru Yang, I assumed, for my inner-weather became overwhelmingly calm with an attendant emotion not quite blissful, no, call it a state of fundamental, genuine happiness.

And this continued like a long silent piece of music, like a visit to the depths of space, suffused with saffron light.

One thought that has especially repeated in me ever since, given the condition I now seem to share with the Guru, is *Follow the silence. Follow the clear light!*

At the sound of the clanging again of his little bronze disks on their leather chord I returned to the Staten Island Ferry as if from a healing sleep. I blinked my eyes. I felt baby-like. New-born.

There sat the Guru across from me. His thin dark face wearing a scowl.

"You poor bastard," he said, the words ringing with concern. "I wouldn't want to move through that mind-stream of yours ever again. Ah. We have all of three minutes left to repair the damage caused by your defensive self-obsessiveness for what? All your twenty-nine years of life?"

MAGIC AND MIRACLES ARE NOTHING SPECIAL,
THEY ONLY COME ALONG ABOUT 13 BILLION TIMES
A DAY

18.
The Guru's Three Minute Special

Guru Yang. This, verbatim, was his diagnosis. I listened. I took notes. I heard.

"You," he began, "have never been blessed to love any one other particular person, Mister Crashaw Pin. Not even, incredibly, Mister Crashaw Pin himself. You have expected boons and they've showered upon you in the form of nurture, education, sexual pleasure, artistic accomplishment. No wonder you can create crazy-seeming poems that reveal brash and forbidden matters, this, yes, this writing alone you have loved. Now there is only one path left to you, for our ferry docks, we have crossed the great water, you are about to encounter the hustle and bustle of New York City. I mean Hustle. And I mean Bustle. Listen: you must renounce it all before you take it up again. You must seek humility, that so devoted friend of ours! You must say to yourself as you enter each room in future, WHAT CAN I DO TO HELP? You have suffered from specialness. From Exceptionalism. Give it up. Give it up, Crashaw Pin, all of it, beginning this instant. You have been wounded in your soul by fear and a desperation for triumph. Peace will never reach you, it's been running along behind trying to catch up with you all this while. Not until you burn out hope and fear will you possess again Your Original Face. Away with the Crashaw, with the wanting, the taking, the relishing. Let in now only what chooses to happen. Let in exclusively the moment. And the next moment. Nothing is real, and yet nothing more precious than what happens. Life is a dream...that HAPPENS. Do not obliterate the moment with your storyline. And if you seek to find me again on this ferry, you'll gain nothing but a nice ride upon the water. I will either not be here, or will be too tied up with another to attend any further with you. Crashaw Pin, I commend you to your own commanding, I command you to begin traversing the long hard transit from I to Eye, from I to Now."

Such were the words of the Guru.

And the ferry gave a long hooting.

19.

Of course it would go beyond the improbable that such an experience could simply place my life thenceforth immediately on another track, as if one might lift and heft a locomotive engine in frail hands to settle it down again ready to travel in an opposite direction. No, not so easy. Not easy at all. But you can stop your damn train from chugging along on its sorry track toward nowhere at ninety-five miles an hour. You pull the chord. You can manage at least to come to a contemplative halt now and then.

20.

After a time in a rented room on 10th Street on the edge of the Village there weren't that many still striving to find me. WHATEVER HAPPENED TO CRASHAW PIN? became a cold case. Over the following years the at first fierce and later modest royalties on *Even Hurry Slowly* piled up. I had this friend who held my P.O. box key passing crucial items along to The Wandering Pin. I figured someday if I became desperate for cash I could always sell my place amid the chickens and switch to a wanderer's backpack.

For a long while, once in Cranbury N.J. again, I avoided my parents' bedroom, the place where they'd made their pillow talk, and love (I hope) and their brave exit. At first I set up a mattress on the first floor of the old house. Eventually I moved up to Mr. Mogul's on the rise we called Chicken Hill. And I let my beard grow. I used a blond wig when I went for supplies in town. The chickens ran wild. I ate a lot of eggs.

And meditated several times a day, for the first three years or so. Now I seem to be meditating all the time, day and night, a thing that happens as if entirely on its own.

For a time, whenever I breathed in after the opening long three breathes I received direct transmission from the Guru. Then not. I was on my own. Recently his voice did briefly return, though shifted up an octave or so, making him sound distinctly female. A brief Guru Yang reappearance, maybe as Guru Yin this time. He/She told me I was doing okay. And to keep going.

A poem of mine, written a bit after the ferry ride, pointed toward this far off result. I was sorry at the time of composition that it hadn't made it into *Even Hurry Slowly*, perhaps as the concluding item.

PATIENCE PRACTICE

no one taught me
patience practice,
it simply began.

I'd wait for each gate to unlock;

maybe a napkin would fall to the floor,
must be picked up, dealt with,
but when?

ANSWER: once that gate
had opened.

Days would go by and suddenly —
stoop.

Years, then suddenly:
insight!

Patience practice:

off with the fuss, the encrusting brocades,
    forget the speed, the Olympian gold.

O, holy creature,
    be exactly
    who you are.

21.

Once missing persons efforts on my behalf subsided, I ventured out a bit further, yet always in disguise. I learned nothing of what became of Goldie, or of our putative child. Working with the Guru by thought-transmission resolved my doubts on the question of parentage. The kid was mine. We are, so Guru's thinking taught me, everybody's father. And then one balmy June morning, out to check the acreage and the winter-fallen spruce, thinking the time had maybe had come to put the place on the market — this was late June, year of our Lord 1999 — I left my front door open as always (what a thing, to live where you needn't lock your door!) and when I returned, there she was, just inside, in a blanket-lined cardboard box. Along with an extra pair of 'jamies, a nippled milk-filled bottle, a packet of diapers, a carton of formula, a tiny, soft hair brush.

The Jim Beam carton also contained an ironic packet of condoms.

There's a well known Zen story about a monk accosted by a girl's parents. "Look what you've done," the parents cry. "You made this baby inside of our girl. Now you must care for it." So the monk nods. In some versions he might even be allowed to say "Ah, so." He cares for the child, and then, two years later, the parents return, all aghast with apologies, for the girl had lied, it wasn't his child after all, and now they wished forgiveness and the baby's return. The monk then hands over the baby. Maybe he even comments "Ah, so."

While warming the bottle supplied I diapered the wet little thing and considered the timing. This, by the way, was my first diapering. Under the circumstance I think I did pretty well. I tested the milk on my arm, put it back in the boiling water, took a pair of scissors and snipped off at the back a tiny bit of the baby's reddish hair. Returned for the milk. My daughter with Goldie would have been what by then? Twenty nine or so. The temp of the bottle felt about right. I lifted her — of course it would be a "her" — wrapped her in the blanket, held her crooked in my arm. I eased the nipple into her mouth. She drank and I held her.

Criticized for carrying a girl
over a stream, a monk says

"I set her body down,
which you still carry."

*

All the bodies
we carry.

I let the gossamer threads of her clipped hair for the DNA sample slip flowing away through my fingers.

113

DWAYNE'S MOVIE

Success has always been the greatest liar.
— *Nietzsche*

WHEN VISITORS ASK DWAYNE HOW he wound up on the mountain, he tends to offer no more than a teasing smile. Actually, he'd reached a rather sad state four years ago around the time of his thirty-third birthday. His most recent temp office job had become very temp thanks to downsizing, so for a while only plastic kept him housed and fed. He felt relegated to a position below the bottom of the food chain, a sort of left-over, his career-description boiling down to ex-con, seldom-employed actor, and terminally luckless writer of screenplays.

In short, he lived in Southern California.

Two weeks before he'd bottomed out, he applied for a waiter's job and wound up as busboy. Of course, like most, he'd waited tables and manned food counters as a kid, but *busboy*, at thirty-three? The night before his birthday he reported rather grudgingly to Dresner's Restaurant & Bar, crowded for a Thursday, featuring a few over-aged Clooney look-alikes (one actually wearing Raybans indoors) along with several pairs of Prada shoes on would-be Prada brides. Dresner's — a fairly classy joint, aspiring to class, anyhow — was slammed that night, diners enjoying, toasting, laughing: a me-too after-theatre crowd. At Dresner's you were meant to believe you'd arrived somewhere. There's hardly a town of reasonable size near Hollywood that fails to support a similar pretend-Manhattan eatery, securely over-priced and

115

under-lit, intending to lift a diner's pride. The black-uniformed, co-ed wait-staff bustled about, trained to keep folded hands behind backs at table-side. These folks were usually actors in disguise, beautiful young people struggling to make it in a beach town painfully close to L.A.

Unlike his youthful colleagues, Dwayne displayed zero enthusiasm for his work, felt out of synch, a kind of one-man *noir* passage amid the evening's color and flash, bending to scoop up dirty dishes and lipstick-stained wine glasses, preparing a table for a group of six late diners waiting nearby. Corinda, his wife of two years, had exchanged him for her yoga instructor. Not without provocation. She'd also made off with most of their so-called communal property. Dwayne's divorce situation was never far from his thoughts, his distraction interrupted by the floor manager who leaned down beside him with comments on his lack of speed and enthusiasm.

"Lipinsky!" he hissed in Dwayne's ear in his authoritatively "foreign" way, "Dwayne, Dwayne, you swear you come with experience!"

"Listen," Dwayne snapped back, "I specified *waiter*-experience! The want ad said *wait-person* and you've stuck me with *busboy*. Not everybody gives great busboy. I'm having trouble accessing my inner-busboy here."

Though essentially a willowy, quizzically-faced actor ripe for comedy, Dwayne at times tried to loom up in a neo-Brando way.

"Wait-person?" the faux-foreign Manager declared, "clean up, *this* is wait-person. Set table — wait-person! What? You want *Assistant Wait-Person*?!"

"Yeah," Dwayne assured him, "Damn straight! Who wouldn't? A trained assistant? Bring her on," and in a sudden rage that surprised even him he set the table as if he were dealing cards in Vegas, an occupation he'd often fantasized. Zip zip, forks here, napkins there, wine glasses glimmering, all nicely if haphazardly arranged. He spun around to head back to the kitchen and this abrupt movement knocked a diner's glass of remnant scotch into his lap.

"Son of a BITCH!" the diner cried.

"I'm terribly sorry, sir." Dwayne attempted to sop up the man's scotch-wet crotch with a snatched napkin.

"*Quit it, quit it, you clumsy fool!*"

The man stood to vibrate his trousers. "You're a lame excuse for a human being, you know that?"

All Dwayne could offer in return was a grave nod, for this remark echoed his own recognition that his life had become something of a disaster. But the scotch-wet diner's female companion spoke more kindly. "It's all right, Sonny," she murmured, "if you'd just bring us a towel and another...hey, wait a second! Babe, look, it's *Uncle Vanya* — right? From Nearly-Third-Street Rep! The Chekhov Fest last season? Honey, our busboy played Uncle Vanya....poor homely Sonia and her Uncle Vanya?" She offered Dwayne a broad smile. "You're much too young and nutty-looking for the part, but you did okay, considering. Hard to see you as a middle-aged Russian, but you made that Vanya loveable. He deserved better than he got, so in love with that awful professor's child bride."

"You didn't recognize him from *Uncle Vanya*, Suze," said her companion. "You recognized him because he's the same kid who spilled water on me the last time we were here." Which Dwayne knew couldn't possibly be true because he'd only worked at Dresner's a total of eight shifts.

Suddenly, incomprehensibly, he found himself removing his apron, stepping back, getting into character. Intense of eye and in his most thunderous if breaking voice he launched into a speech from *Vanya*, not from his own role but repeating the words of the peevish professor, Vanya's nemesis. A hush settled over the restaurant as Dwayne acted-out among the tables.

"*I am not stupid and I understand! You are young, healthy, beautiful, you want to live, and I'm an old man, almost a corpse. Well?*"

Well? Of course it is stupid of me to go on living!"

A beat; all eyes focused on him, or so it seemed. But then the diners appeared essentially bewildered and as if on cue fell back to their food and drink.

Dwayne held his pose, apron clutched histrionically in a fist flung high. "Ah, fuck it," he declared, "gotta know when to fold 'em!" He spiked the apron to the floor and made his exit. Several diners actually applauded in a half-hearted way.

So what next? What exactly could he do, newly jobless again, ex-busboy, thirty-three? He returned morosely to his post-divorce studio apartment with its small-sized refrigerator, hot plate, the floor littered with newspapers and mail, a plank desk in the corner supporting a vintage Dell computer and a tall-ish pile of accumulated *New Yorkers*, the walls hung with cult movie posters.

His digital clock blinked to 12:01. He popped on his rabbit-eared TV and searched his pockets for a cigarette, removing from the little fridge a chocolate Hostess Cupcake with white squiggly frosting. Cupcake in hand, cigarette in mouth, he moved to his skuzzy couch, plopped down and considered the tiny TV screen, which displayed several near-naked Japanese runners trudging up a mountain trail.

He lit the cigarette and stuck it in the cupcake as if it were a candle, filter-end down. Then he blew on the lighted tip. Then he sang, in imitation of Tom Waits' gravelly voice, the first line only of "Happy Birthday to me."

The striving runners on the TV screen wore loincloths as they stumbled through rugged terrain. Each scarcely clad aspirant carried a dagger tucked into his diaper-like running shorts. A Voice-Over supplied commentary: "...fifty miles, night after night, these men seek enlightenment. Their daggers? For the suicide they vow to commit if ever they fail to complete their grueling runs."

It took Dwayne several blasts of breath above the cupcake, but at last he made his cigarette-candle briefly blaze. He clicked off the overhead light to settle down, finding the next morning that the cigarette-candle in the birthday cup cake had burned down to its filter, a wide trace of ash across the frosting.

As it happened, this day would prove a life-changer for Dwayne. It started with drowsy coffee-making as he took a few dabs at straightening up the place. A joyful Dwayne Lipinsky was still buried away within him somewhere, entombed by weight of circumstance. But how to let that cheerier version out? As a self-help fan, among volumes of perky advice accumulated in his brick and board bookcase he often turned to Dwight Johnson's MAKE IT SING with its repeated notion that *wanting* prevents *having*. If you "dream," as the ubiquitous American word had it, you can't *ipso facto* be awake, or so Johnson preached. You miss what's happening in the here and now because you're off in the future striving for gain, closure, love, more love. Dwayne's friend and fellow con Zak Bremmer — an unrepentant Texan who'd been moonlighting as a gumshoe for a private detective agency before prison claimed him for a stretch longer than Dwayne's – Zak at times called Dwayne *Igor*, after Dr. F's lumbering assistant, played so magnificently by Marty Feldman (YOUNG FRANKINSTEIN). Zak, with whom Dwayne shared a cell for over three years, was a kind of role-model for him, a fearless fuck-up. Dwayne could only aspire to such self-assertive confidence.

After lunch he wandered about, thinking that later he might get right to work applying for another rip-off temp office job. Strolling down Rodriguez Street, the town's spine, he drifted into a bookstore, Maxim's Books & Music, and stood ironically in front of the Self Help section. He pulled a title from the shelf: *JUST F-ING DO IT! The Procrastinator's Handbook.* He thumbed through this thin volume and damned if he didn't turn up, among the photographs in the central section, three images of the Japanese multi-night 50-mile runners. He slipped the book

119

into his jacket pocket, then left the store, moving distractedly amid the foot traffic of visitors and local people passing the heavy ceremonial bronze doors of the Saks Fifth Avenue branch a few doors down from Maxim's. From the look of the tourists strolling around him they'd rather be shopping at one of the places farther south that featured tee-shirts reading: *My Other Lover Is Godzilla, How Can You Fucking Compete?!* or *I'll Blow (Up) Anybody*!

As lower Rodriguez began to drift into the condition of a sailor's town, Dwayne paused before a junk arcade — junk offered as "antiques" — and entered. The long shop was filled with vintage stuff: antiquated tools, Tiffany-like lamps, books, clocks, hat-stands, hats. He poked around toward the front and found himself focused on a dagger nested on the top shelf of a locked octagonal glass display case, lying there amid fake gem-studded watches and Victorian medallions. A pretty, small-featured shopgirl, Modigliani neck and improbably copious blonde dreadlocks, unlocked the display case for him and fetched out the dagger, partially inserted in a scratched brown leather sheath. The girl stood waiting, dangling her keys. She was California-slim, with a delicately aristocratic face. The weapon sported a horse's head at the end of its brass handle and was tagged "Moroccan, old, $60.00."

She watched Dwayne in a deliberately amused way. She had clear blue eyes and a flawless complexion. Not that he looked at her that closely, busy studiously running a finger back and forth along the dagger's dullish blade and testing its broken tip. He wondered if the Japanese spiritual-exercise runners would put up with a laughable dagger like this. This dagger would barely pierce an apple. He mimed to the girl a bit of comic-frustration at being unable to cut anything with it.

"There's that meat market up on Questa, they sharpen stuff for free."

He rubbed his wrist against the blade with a manic laugh. He'd buy it anyway, for symbolic value. "Ah," he said, "they'll sharpen, but then you're expected to buy some meat, which I don't exactly need."

She smiled, tilted her head and shrugged her shoulders charmingly. He was left holding the dagger as she slipped away for the moment to deal with another customer.

Only then did he realize — with a double-take — that she was Adriana! Of course. He caught up with her toward the rear of the shop.

"Adriana! You were my student! Look, look how you've...filled out!"

"I knew you wouldn't remember me, Mr. Lipinsky. That must've been what? Three years ago?" She brightened. "I saw you in Chekhov at the Rep. You were so *good!* I actually went and read that play, *Uncle Vanya*. What a sad man. Hey, congratulations! I've done some local theater myself, nothing major but that's okay, because I'm really into painting now, I share a studio with my step-sisters, you should come see my stuff. Will you? I'm painting huge these days, 9 x 12, can you believe it?" And then she struck a rapt pose and spoke improbably in Chekhov's words:

"My poor, poor Uncle Vanya, you are crying! You have never known happiness, but wait, Uncle Vanya, wait! We shall rest. We shall rest. We shall rest."

"Incredible, you've memorized Sonia's lines!"

"...just more or less that one speech."

"Ah...you work here? Last time I saw you, gosh, you were the bright hope of 11th grade English.

"We must work, Uncle...work for others without rest."

She beamed in contained amusement. After a pause she stared at him with a wondering smile. "You're interested in daggers?" And then, with force: "I can't believe you didn't remember me! Is it the dreadlocks?"

"I'm a little distracted these days, Adriana. You don't want to hear about it."

"Well, we'll always have the 11th grade."

121

He had to laugh. So young to be flirting *Casablanca*-style. Adorable. But even if there weren't — what? — a dozen or more years between them…if, in another dispensation, he might actually have been her contemporary, would he have had a chance with a girl like Adriana?

Saddened, with a jaunty wave, he left the arcade, clutching his little bag containing the Moroccan dagger she'd sold him, imagining her observing him through the front window as he moved along down Rodriguez toward the beach, figuring to return to his dreary flat, maybe spend the rest of his birthday catching up on his great cache of unread *New Yorker*s.

He walked along carrying the bag with the dysfunctional dagger, inwardly distraught.

Shit, he thought, *this is just too heartlessly sad.*

How had he become Adriana's teacher? While serving out every single day of his three year four month drug-grower's sentence at Saldana, he did a lot of work toward his B.A. in Education, and when Southern California became especially hungry for substitute teachers, he'd managed to pick up a temporary certificate, obscuring his criminal history. For a time.

We'll always have the 11th grade.

He thought about her while drowsing in his apartment, going through the *New Yorker* cartoons from back to front, drowsing again, then another *New Yorker*. Suddenly he threw down the magazine in hand and briskly paced through town to reach the main drag and reenter Adriana's shop, screwing up his courage, reaching for some perkiness, taking a chance, making his move. He asked for her position on lunch, how she felt regarding the institution of lunch?

The institution of lunch, she told him with a laugh, had her complete approval. She was madly in favor of lunch.

"Then how would it be," he enquired, "if I bought you some late lunch, somewhere nice? To make up for not at first recognizing a young woman so clearly…recognizable? I've already had lunch myself, of course, but I could watch you enjoying yours, plus as your former teacher I could maybe slip you a few eating pointers."

"Really? Lunch? Sometime next week would be best. I was just teasing before, you know, Mr. Lipinsky, about your strangely forgetting me."

"Please." he spoke calmly, with dignity. "Call me Dwayne. And lunch has to be today. That's because, okay, today's my birthday — what about that?!"

"Wow. Rare. My step-dad Roger's in back, he can take over. Hey, I'm going on a late lunch-date with my old substitute teacher!"

"Not *that* old, Adriana. You choose the place. I'll order dessert for me. Maybe I'll even tell you the sad story of what happened when I connected with that actor Krasinski."

"Oh, I love sad stories! Let's go to Dresner's, that's my fave."

She moved to the back to talk to her step-Dad while he appreciated her small rear end with a degree of what can only be called reverence. She returned with a smile. How appealing she seemed, her unmarked face with its pale-red lipstick, her lithe body in a flimsy chiffon blouse under a black sweater, her near-scandalous shop-girl miniskirt. There's probably a municipal ordinance, Dwayne thought, against advanced-Lolitas like Adriana. He realized that he had to keep his libidinal interests carefully at bay. Maybe he'd tell her the story of his disconnect with DeVito, the diminutive actor bailing on the supporting role of a lifetime, DeVito and director Kramer and the damned Krasinski guy and of course his own battered, favorite script. Maybe he'd even regale her with a comic approach to his divorce-fiasco.

Dresner's, even in uncrowded daylight, remained dark, quite *New Yorkaise.* They occupied a booth up front, across from the vast mirror behind the gaudily stocked walnut bar. The daytime staff failed to recognize Dwayne, dressed for birthday in olive-colored suit and yellow-blue necktie. Adriana ordered a marguerita and he treated himself to a martini with house gin and olives. The waiter at first hesitated, hands folded behind his back, for the girl must have looked to him terribly young. Dwayne observed the man deciding for the sake of amiability not to check her age, recognizing this fellow though the waiter failed to know him (busboys are invisible).

Dwayne was busy striving to calm his eroticized mind by soaking up light banter with Adriana. But gradually the glow of flirtation dimmed. In fact, all turned rather somber, serious, something meaningful in the way the two of them fell into silent glances, awkwardly wondering almost-smiles. They hovered in an atmosphere of hesitation. He found himself sounding rather avuncular.

"Sonya dear, listen, are you sure you're old enough to drink so much alcohol so quickly in the early afternoon?"

"If you're young enough for daggers, Uncle Ivan, I'm old enough for margaritas. They never card me in here. Hey, I'm practically twenty-one anyhow."

She was without question too young for him.

But if he made inspired moves? If he became instantly a better, more worthy human being, authentically charming, would the thirteen-some years of distance in their ages become bridgeable somehow? No. Her elfin beauty wouldn't go well with his sense of defeat. Impossible. Yet this recognition in no way assuaged the yearning for her that had begun with the unexpected glimmerings of vitality in their initial conversation at the antiques arcade. Such a lustful admiration he'd felt for her bright smile, the ridiculous blond dreadlocks surrounding her small face, her gently curving nose...not to mention the daring skirt plus her flimsy India-print top mostly concealed under the light, black sweater. *And her humor, Dwayne? And her smarts?* In this manner he chastised himself. *You somehow have neglected to add qualities of soul to the list of attractions.*

124

Dwayne shook his head, felt a shiver run through his body. An impossible situation.

Desperate to lift the mood at the restaurant, he declared that he was about to tell her a Jewish joke. "Okay?" he asked. "I happen to know this one awful Jewish joke."

Already amused, she nodded consent.

"Right. Joke. Abe asks Sam, 'What looks like a lox, it's shaped like a box, and it whistles?' So Sam says 'What's shaped like a box and it whistles? What? Tell already.' So Abe says: 'A flying lox-box! No, wait, I mean *whistles*. A lox-box that whistles. Flying, that's another joke.' 'A lox-box? That's your answer?' 'Sure. It's shaped like a box, it's a lox-box, what else?' 'But Abe, Abe, a *flying* lox box...?' 'Not flying, that was a mistake.' 'Okay, but a lox-box that *whistles*? What's with the whistles?' 'That I put in,' says Abe, 'so you shouldn't guess.' "

"Dwayne," said Adriana, "I love you. You're out of your fuckin' mind."

She gazed at him with a look that could have passed for enjoyment but which at that moment he preferred to interpret as involving the early stages of adoration.

No, he realized, what she was feeling was mild amusement, tinged with a bit of surprise.

"That joke happens to be the story of my life, Adriana. I look like a Dwayne, I'm shaped like a Dwayne...granted I don't fly, but hey, I *whistle so you shouldn't guess*. I wove that very riddle-joke into a film-script once, the one script of mine that was incredibly nearly making it until it absolutely *didn't*, needless to say. Great excitement followed by grave despair. The story of my life. One long *expungement*. At least I've learned to abandon hope and pack away the script in my Emily Dickinson drawer."

"I want to read it."

"What?"

"The screenplay you packed away."

"You do?"

"Does a lox-box whistle?"

So they moved out into the early evening, strolling to his apartment to get the script, continuing over to the downtown branch of the library, where Adriana moved steadily through its early pages. Unlettered laborers at tables nearby humbly accepted whispered teachings from helpful ladies on illiteracy patrol. Children smiled at each other with gleeful, guilty looks: they had an angle on how to view pornography on the computers set up in the magazine section. Harried mothers checked out vast numbers of thin, over-sized kiddie-books in hopes of a free moment some day just to themselves. And Adriana looked ardently up from her reading. In library-appropriate whispers she said to Dwayne: "I think it's wonderful."

"Really?! Wonderful?" He blurted this much too loudly for a library, then lowered his volume to a whisper. "And you haven't even hit page 44 where the singing monkey comes in with his sexual demands! No, no, that's another script. Not really. Another joke. Joke, joke, my bad habit, I do jokes when I get excited."

A few pages further along Adriana insisted she'd even take her comment beyond *wonderful* — all the way to *excellent*. She told Dwayne that she loved how Custer, the story's young hero, kept failing at managing to kill himself. The kid in the script (NAKED, ON A NAKED HORSE, IN THE POURING RAIN) had fallen so low he couldn't even manage to shuffle off his mortal coil. He tried a gun, but while gazing into a bathroom mirror he slipped on wet tile and consequently blasted not his skull but his own reflection in the glass, seven years additional bad luck ("a darkened comedy" is the phrase Dwayne used to pitch this screenplay during the one amazing period when it received serious attention from Names in the business).

The Custer character then rented a ride on a sight-seeing Piper Cub, planning to jump out, but got caught on his seat-belt, causing the disgusted pilot to tug him back in (a tricky scene to film) saying "Damn these college kids, can't they leap from a freeway overpass or something?"

Dwayne's hero — named after the disaster-prone hot-shot General at Little Big Horn — next stuffed the door cracks in his parents' garage and turned on the CO_2 in the family's Buick, slumping down at last in the front seat and thus lurching the gear-lever into reverse, which slammed him right back out through crunched garage doors to conclude against a telephone pole at the curb.

Undaunted, young Custer rented himself a kayak, rolled it over in the sea with himself weighted-down and tightly harnessed within. Bubbles rose...until some interfering Do-Gooder on a water scooter righted him again to CPR him on the beach and pass him on to a certain Dr. Dunkle who sat conveniently nearby reading under a black beach-umbrella.

This is where Adrianna paused to offer further praise, for she'd reached a key plot-point where Dwayne's protagonist actually takes out a contract on himself with Dr. Dunk, a mob-contract, seeing that he obviously needed help with his suicide.

It appeared that the story managed to be both whimsical and sad enough for Adriana to adore it. At least that's what she said. "I adore it, Dwayne. Especially him! What happens next? I want to be his *mother*!"

What happened next with the script was that through friends of friends the story miraculously reached the hands of an authentic hot and youngish director of the day, Aldo Kramer (ULTIMATE FRISBEE; MIRNA AND HER BROTHERS). Dwayne imagined Kramer as he page-turned, invented a scene right out of a sexy B-role: hot tub just off a terrace, wet bar nearby, stately mountains in the distance, stands of bamboo, Buddha statuary, the works, plus three Buxoms who provided giggles and splashes and pneumatic bliss in the tub where Kramer had become, in Dwayne's imagining, entirely lost in the story and so insanely enthusiastic that he rudely pushed the bevy of tubbed beauties aside, speaking in Ratso Ritso fashion without looking up from the wet page in his hand.

KRAMER
I'm reading here! I'm reading here!

The director's eyes would have lit up particularly at the point where Custer tried again to kill himself, this time by starvation, and wandered off through a forest in his wet suit after the kayak scene...only to spook the horse of a girl (there's always a girl) who joined him in trying to break the contract with Dr. Dunkle (a perfect part for Danny DeVito). Dwayne could see the diminutive actor actually playing the hell out of this role. Director Aldo Kramer already had some wonderful casting ideas: Maria Sorbelle for the girl on the horse (who runs a health food restaurant), John Krasinski for Custer, brilliant notion there, and it all had become overwhelmingly real, till things got even better, for John Cleese's documentary production company took an interest: this would be their first fiction film; Cleese considered the Dunkle role for himself, wild, a stunning development, and then — can you believe it?! — Kramer died. The director was mildly into his forties yet he upped and died. Forty-three years old – an embolism — unbearable. And two days later Cleese pulled out, and of course Krasinski did as well, all in a row, all gone, take that, and of course the Custer-project proceeded to die entirely and Dwayne realized then more fully than ever that he'd become truly, deeply jinxed. He decided to set the damned script aside, didn't want to think about it, look at it. Why continue to strive when the world clearly has it in for you?

It's 4:47 p.m. in the downtown branch of the library as Adriana enquires with a baffled look: "You never tried to shop the property again?"

"Naw, I received a message. Who needs the pain? You know how they say 'No' in Hollywood? They say 'Yes.' "

She touched his hand. "I love you, Dwayne. You're completely sui-generous. Wait, wait, it's here in my handbag somewhere. A surprise. About your wonderful script. That you just gave up on. Oh my. Granted, you took a little trauma, but just to give up?!"

She fetched a folded page from the depths of her bag. Dwayne unfolded it as she smiled knowingly across from him. The page was from the magazine *FilmFlams* and it announced a generous offer from Steven Spielberg intending to encourage first time film-writers.

The page revealing the Spielberg contest trembled in Dwayne's hand.

The generous offer proposed that three winning contestants each year would have scripts *made*, from pre-production through distribution, on an Indie budget of up to 6 mil., with personal hands-on attention from senior Spielberg staff, including efforts, if appropriate, to involve A-list performers in cameos, and with the winning writers learning all aspects of the collaborative art of film-making by hanging out daily with production and post-production, involved even during the distribution process from first till last. Dwayne had completely missed catching sight of this opportunity.

"Wow, Adriana," was all he could say. "The deadline's, hmm, let's see, oh gosh, Tuesday, December 9th, that's just a week from next Tuesday!"

But he really had no worry about deadlines, for the Custer script was already written, in fact rewritten scores of times. Except that entering a contest would involve setting himself up once more for either winning or losing. Dangerous *to want*, to expect, to feel hungry, to express desire.

Oddly enough, something quite similar happens in the Custer-movie, namely a great shift in young Custer's intent, for once he'd signed on for professional help in exiting the human condition came what can only be described as an immense change-of-heart. There's documentation for this sort of thing: death looms up super real and, SHAZAM, life becomes even more so. Thus the Custer story shifts in Act Two into a non-stop series of adventures as the kid runs away from his hit-man Dr. Duncle. Yes, as soon as he'd signed up for a death by contract, arranged to have himself zapped, a stupendous interest in every breath, in every precious little thing swelled up within, particularly since he (Custer) had left college to go to work for beautiful Angie (Marie Sorbelle) at the health-food restaurant. O beautiful world!

Dwayne stared at Adriana across the library table. Could she be his health-food-Angie? Devoted to making his life come unbelievably right?

The brochure promised the selection of the first year's winning scripts no later than end-February.

Could a guy put off self-mutilating plans until then?

Why not?

"So," Adriana whispered, "you'll send your script to the contest and cultivate a more up-beat attitude?"

"I will, I will, I'm going to hit a quick final draft and make the damn thing perfect by Tuesday!"

"You actually *are* cheering up. I can see it right before mine eyes! Oh, Uncle Ivan," she said, "do it!"

By early morning Monday, three days later, Dwayne found himself clicking at his computer's keyboard, feeling just about his best since boyhood. He saw his new friend Adriana daily, she served as mentor on the revisions of the Custer script, tumbling over with ideas. She kept jotting notes, giving Dwayne notes, he was rewriting, tightening, the script would be ready by the deadline, maybe would even be found worthy of the eyes of Steven

Spielberg and staff.

In his little studio apartment Dwayne propped the "Do It!" book he'd stolen on the shelf above his desk. In its pages he'd rediscovered the Japanese consecrated spiritual runners with their daggers. These practitioners were described at some length as they covered fifty-mile courses no matter snow, regret, or pneumonia. Dwayne could imagine what they had to contend with. The book described sleet storms along steep trails as the holy runners transported their galloping cases of exhaustion for fifty miles, and then the next night fifty again, plodding ahead, pushing on — well, good for them, they'd serve as role-models for him in his perfecting of the Custer script for Spielberg.

Spiffing up the screenplay, he'd reached the point where Custer turns his weighted kayak bottoms-up, where even the music goes silent and you hear the sea-surge and the gull-cry with the beach deserted late in the day. All the little kids are back home by then, their hair starched from the salt ocean, playing Monopoly or working with their Lego bricks, the Mommies maybe dressing for the evening or Dads doing barbeque. Next the water-skier comes along like a save-the-world helicopter, spots the overturned kayak, grabs supine, suicidal Custer and gives him CPR on the gleaming wet sand as the sun dips away, maybe that's what Custer and Dwayne had wanted all along, just to take self-destruction that far and no further, to see if one of God's little angels would appear and initiate a turn in the expungement story.

INT. SPIELBERG'S OFFICE SUITE – DAY

Dwayne sits in a lushly appointed waiting area eyeing several others among the large group perched nearby. Money for administration in the Spielberg contest apparently flowed freely, with folks ferried in from all over the country for interviews and consultation, expenses paid. Adriana, settled next to him, surreptitiously held his hand for comfort and reassurance.

131

Among those waiting to be interviewed, Dwayne had already taken a special interest in NADIA, a homely dark-haired woman (bangs, horn-rims, dowdy dress); FRANKIE, a cow-licked guy who looked about seventeen though actually, as it turned out, was firmly in his 40's — he stared straight ahead, his face contracted to a mad grimace of meditative concentration — and RAOUL, 25-ish, clearly French from the sniffy expression on his elegant, upper-crust puss.

Nadia's hands were folded, Raoul snobbed the world with narrow face and narrow, permanently arched brows, arms crossed at his narrow chest. Frankie, eyes staring agleam as if burning in an onslaught of drugs, actually spent the waiting room time with legs folded on his chair in meditative posture.

One at a time, various script contestants were invited to enter the conference room beyond. Some returned to the waiting area with triumphant expressions, others downcast, offering an instant read on the way they imagined their interview to have gone.

And finally Dwayne was called.

Adriana nudged him alert to what was happening.

He entered the conference room and, unbelievably, faced *Steven Spielberg,* flanked by several SUITS sitting one beside the other in Supreme Court fashion behind a long table set up like a barrier under the windows.

Stephen Spielberg, imagine!

Dwayne felt unbelievably tense.

Director Spielberg consulted a sheaf of notes. "Please," he said, "have a seat, Mr. ... um. Coffee? Make yourself comfortable, we want to get a sense of your background, your aspirations, that sort of thing...we expect to work closely every day with the winning writers for a year or more — are you feeling okay? You seem somehow...

DWAYNE
I can't believe this! This is great.

132

(declaratively)
You're Steven Spielberg!

SPIELBERG
(amused)

I am.

"Actually," said one of the several executive in the room, "sorry to disappoint but it's his clone, actually. You seldom get to see real celebrities anymore, it's all either look-alikes or these outrageous clones."

"We're just a wee bit exhausted by now," said Spielberg. "But tell us about your work. You've survived a first mass filtering, that's quite some progress. I congratulate you. Now, we can't each say we have a crystal-clear recollection of your project, since we've spread the initial readings around, but somebody put you in this select group."

"Steven, isn't it drinkee-pooh time?" asked one of the two middle-aged women in the room. "Can't we open another bottle of wine while we field this pitching? I think we'd really better offer Dwayne here a glass, he looks so in awe I'm afraid he may break apart."

"Thank you," said Dwayne, "I'd be ecstatic for a touch of wine."

"You are sort of loveable though underfed, Mr. Dwayne. May I take you home after our interrogation?"

Spielberg signaled to an underling sitting off at the rear and the fellow proceeded to open wine bottles and produce canapés and glasses. They were all feeling terminally silly except for Dwayne. He remained amazed and aroused. The group offered various toasts to the end of a long session of interviews. "To the great art of Cin-em-a." "To mindlessly generous Steven." "Let's drink to Dwayne...to Dwayne's movie!" The underling who poured the wine began to play the stand-up piano across the room. He sang, in a fine, Irish tenor, "The Bluebird of Happiness."

Spielberg smiled a what-can-you-do sort of smile.

Back in the waiting room Adriana asked how the interview had gone and Dwayne just shook his head. But the next day he received a phone call from Spielberg's executive secretary. The woman said: "Mr. Spielberg asked me to mention that you made quite an impression on the prize committee as a good sport when they fell into a late-in-the-day tizzy, and he assures you that they will each and all read your screenplay ON A NAKED HEARSE and give it serious consideration."

At which point Dwayne honestly didn't know whether to shriek for joy or go hang himself because of the tension.

Three days later Adriana raced into his place holding the mail from his box, crying *A letter from the Spielberg Contest!*

Dwayne's apartment was a lot neater then before. It had clearly felt a woman's hand.

Adriana and Dwayne looked at the letter.

They turned it this way and that.

Minutes passed.

The letter sat unopened, leaning against the clock on the mantel.

At last both of them approached the thing through an ominous silence on the soundtrack.

They tossed the letter nervously back and forth like a hot-potato-object from a Marx Brothers routine.

Finally Adriana tore it open. With a shriek: *We're in the cut-down, the final cut-down!*

And so they danced about, and so did the letter, flying from hand to hand as if it were a helium party balloon.

What happened next? Can you guess? Here's Spielberg talking to Dwayne face to face: "You're the *only* official standby, Dwayne. You came that close! I'm really sorry, I had to speak to you directly. We'll turn to the standby if we run into creative differences with any of the winners. Not likely, granted, but you have a useful fall-back role. If a winner's not able to devote full time to hanging in with our process as we've devised it…hey, people have been known to withdraw even from prize-winning situations, maybe they'll go shopping for a better deal, who knows, but if so, there you'd be, standing by as *The Standby*, ready to fill in, it's not such a bad deal."

Dwayne felt as if he were in the midst of a key scene from NAKED, ON A NAKED HORSE, IN THE POURING RAIN, the big re-enactment of the Battle of Little Big-Horn, with him playing the role of the historic Custer in general's uniform. An Apache ambush explodes, there's carnage all around, actor-Indians kill remnants of Custer's troops and the Apache about to scalp Dwayne-as-Custer appears to be wielding an *actual* tomahawk!

The horse-headed dagger Dwayne had purchased from Adriana back in November, lifted from the wall where it had resided above his computer and the *Do It!* book, is now clutched in Dwayne's fist. And this on the very day when Dwayne received a visit from his old cell-mate Zak, Zak out at last on parole, bunking with Dwayne in a bedroll on the apartment floor while Dwayne raged, dagger in hand, at the disappointment of winding up, once again, a standby. Zak listened to his old cellmate. Now and then he threw disgusted glares and glances Dwayne's way. A day later they strolled along the sea-edge, barefoot, dodging thin squiggles of tar, pausing to collect flat stones containing intriguing holes. Here and there they passed a sun-baking girl and stopped to contemplate. The air was early-March, cool, invigorating, the Pacific…*pacific.*

Dwayne and Zak discussed the Spielberg situation.

"Listen, m'man," said Zak, tall and country, white now at the temples, "you gotta love your dream, go for it, everybody says so. It's all over the TV. Fuck! Standby! Incredible. We need a plan."

They were splashing, pants legs rolled, in and out of the water.

"What they say a lot in the self-help books is you like give up everything," Dwayne told him, "and then you just go on doing it anyhow, but it's like *different*. Like if you stopped pursuing

135

happiness, maybe it would catch up with you instead of just running along behind all the time, you know? Trying to catch up? As you rush ahead?"

"Yeah?" said Zak. "Listen, tell me something, you're depressed, right? About not winning that stupid script contest? "

"Sure. Anybody'd be discouraged to wind up the way I always do."

"Listen, compadre, about that I have a great idea, a Majoro Moment is about to arrive."

"Shit, Zak, to have come so close! Better never to have loved at all than to miss by a hair. Don't you think? To come within a lousy hair…"

'Within a lousy *hair*? Spare me, Dwayne. Within a lousy murder, you mean."

"Say what?"

Dwayne literally began to tremble. "Zak," he told his friend, "you are one crazy mother!"

"But it's sooo simple. That gal of yours, that Adriana? She's setting up to save your ass, isn't that right? So just how intimate has that scene become? Ha. Thought so. Listen, once we get you beyond *Standby*, impressionable girls being what they are, who knows, man, you might even reap some ultimate reward from that cutie. *Reap*! Dwayne, hear what I'm saying? I'm talkin' *girl*, I'm talkin' *reap*, and you just go on specializing in woe!"

Dwayne tried to take this in.

"Dude, what's a Standby for? To fill in, man. To fill in for somebody who fails to show, who can't constantly stay on the scene and learn the movie business because, as I'm trying to explain, they're already dead, so in comes MR. STANDBY! Wake up! You'd only need to whack the one. One out of three."

"This is a joke, Zak — right? A guy has to be a killer to get ahead?"

"That's the American way. You gotta love your dream, gotta go for it, everybody says so. Fuck! Anybody can be president, we all know that. Except for ex-cons."

A major point. Dwayne tried to take it in.

"One of three!" Dwayne began to laugh and sweat both. "Wouldn't want to get into serial-killing script-writers. C'mon, Zak. We actually *kill* one of the winners?"

"Exactly! You. You kill. That's the sum total truth and the only option at this point and I and everybody else must know that's true."

"I'm not the type, Zak. Bad casting. I'm more the sort of guy who whacks himself."

At which point his buddy glared at him and gave him the finger. "*Farrr-roock* you, Dwayne! You going anywhere the way you're going? — the way you just let yourself be fucked over by your damned whadda-ya-call-it, *expungements*? Here comes a friend with a generous idea of how to take care of who's standing in the way, and what does this friend receive for his trouble? Admiration? Gratitude? Nah. Cynicism."

DWAYNE
(in a cracked whisper)
A murder? Seriously?

ZAK
Toss a coin, which of the three.

DWAYNE
Goodbye to old loser Dwayne, by God.

ZAK
You'd be a killer, Igor. The girl will
love you. Trust me. You want to spend the
rest of your life as a Standby? I know how
these things work. Violence in a good cause
is downright patriotic.

To this very day Dwayne feels deeply ashamed of what happened next, but as if in a bad dream he rather shortly found himself in a bookstore in Cambridge, Massachusetts, the workplace of script-writer Nadia Senn. It hadn't taken long for Zak to discover the addresses of the winners at Spielberg's place. The bookstore where Nadia worked would be the key. Zak felt certain that Dwayne could get the woman alone for the hit via bookstore chat. He knew Dwayne would give exceptionally good *bookstore*.

A tasteful tag read *Nadia* at the shoulder of the woman Dwayne approached asking for help in finding a copy of JUST F-ING DO IT, the self-help book he already owned. He mentioned to her — as if she wouldn't have known already — that her name in Russian meant *hope*.

"Yes," she agreed, watchfully amused. "A hard name to live up to."

He had to get her completely alone, super conscious of the bulge of Zak's ankle-pistol in his back pocket, a gun weighing roughly five ounces, pearl-handled.

He and Zak and Adriana had settled a few hours earlier at a bed & breakfast place on Ellery Street where each had a separate small room, a shared bath at the end of the hall. This was a fine old-fashioned Cambridge house, French windows downstairs, a sitting area looking out on a small late March garden. They'd rented a Budget Chevy at Logan, zapped through the tunnel and along Storrow Drive, and then Zak, to keep Adriana occupied, prepared to drive the two of them out for some sight-seeing at the bridge in Concord/Lexington where the most useful of American wars had begun. Meanwhile Dwayne would set up the Nadia-hit at Harvard Booksellers, a short block from Brattle Square.

"What's the purpose of this trip?" Adriana wanted to know. "Why would she want to withdraw as a contest-winner?"

Ah, Zak and Dwayne assured her, wait and see.

It's at this point — and it's hateful to report — that while Dwayne was making lit-talk with victim Nadia Senn, Zak made moves on Adriana, and not for the first time. She told Dwayne the whole story months later, wanting to be sure he knew how deftly, how much in her Jane Austen mode, she'd rejected Zak's advances in their little rented Chevy there in still-snowbound Lexington after she and Zak had taken a quick look at the bridge famed for the shot heard round the world. Cold. Zak passed her his flask, the whiskey tasting like flame. She took a good long hit. Then he settled beside her in the Chevy's back seat.

"What are you doing, Zak?"

"Thought you might enjoy a toke 'a this."

He held out a joint.

Adriana hesitated, then toked. "Oh, good! What *is* this stuff?"

"Old fashioned Panama Red."

"We didn't bring the right clothes. It's *freezing*. Better get back to Cambridge. Dwayne will worry about us."

Zak put a clip on the joint and passed it back to her. "Mmm," she said and scrunched down, closing her eyes. "I still don't understand what Dwayne could possibly offer that woman to get her to withdraw and give him her place. Let's hit it back to the B & B, Zak."

She wanted to return him to the driver's seat again so she could safely nap in the rear. But he came closer instead.

Zak and Adriana...she was a little drunk, of course, a little stoned, and he was more than a little crude, kissing her hair, her brow, oh no, but she assured Dwayne when she told the story that something like Wonder Woman rose up in her. "Zak! Please!" Zak extricated himself, muttering "Maybe when it's warmer, back at the B & B? Tonight? When you're in a better mood?"

"This has absolutely nothing to do with mood, you bastard. Some friend you are to Dwayne!"

"Oh, so you belong to Dwayne now, do you? Bullshit, Adriana. Bullshit!"

But he moved around to the driver's seat, murmuring "That was the shot unheard around the world."

"You *know* how he feels about me. Don't pretend you don't, Zak. I should never have come along on this insane trip, much less get Roger and my mother to pay for it. Listen, let's pretend nothing happened out here between us. If you don't say a word, I won't either."

But of course eventually she did tell the story to Dwayne, who had no choice but to credit her version, that Zak started the car and took her, Miss Daisy fashion, back from Lexington to Cambridge in a heavy silence, muttering to himself now and then incomprehensibly.

Meanwhile, at the bookstore, Nadia told Dwayne that she remembered him from the reception room at Spielberg's office suite.

DWAYNE
Nice. I thought you could...maybe teach me
something about script-writing? I wanted so
much to talk with a *success,* a winner. Maybe
study a script like yours. Somewhere in private?

NADIA
(encouraging smile)
You wanted to have a chat with me...
about my documentary?

DWAYNE
(pulling up short)
It's a documentary?!

NADIA
Well, it's about women script-writers,
so very coarsely treated by Hollywood.
These four women sell their bodies to

finance an exposé. It's funny too. Not
really a documentary, what they call
"faux," like it pretends…

DWAYNE
I know "faux," I know "faux"! Sorry,
listen: can we just go somewhere…
to talk? Just us? I have to confess,
I'm a little, just a little — how do you
say? — *smitten* with you, from those
times in the waiting room at Spielberg's?

NADIA
How sweet…but the girl with you there,
holding your hand…?

DWAYNE
(*swiftly*)
My sister. My little sister.

NADIA
Oh.

DWAYNE
She knew I was nervous so she…

NADIA
…she came along?

EXT. RAMSHAKLED HOUSE – NIGHT

A 60's style VW van chugs to a stop outside a house in Arlington,
Mass. as Nadia emerges from the driver's seat and Dwayne from
the passenger's side.

141

NADIA
Well, here it is. Have you had any
supper, you poor man?

The two of them ascend a precarious staircase to the sagging front porch of a three-story house.

Meanwhile, back at the B & B, on the second and somewhat slanty floor of a place obviously built for people of a tidier size than Zak, Dwayne's once ex-con friend had to duck his head as he moved stealthily along the hallway to reach Door #3. Adriana's door.

"Addie," he whispered hoarsely, "You awake in there? Playing with yourself?"

Night-lights already gleamed at either end of the hall, casting garish shadows. No response from Door #3. Zak tapped lightly again with his long fingernails and Adriana called out: "Get the fuck away from my door!"

"I thought we could try again, take a different approach... while we're waiting for Dwayne?"

Through the chained-door opening appeared her nose and mouth.

"I'm a virgin, Zak. Did you realize? Now, if you were me, would you want to give it up to a person like you?"

"Well, ha, wow, I see your point, Sweetie...only I totally don't believe you."

"Wanna come in and check it out?"

"I donno, kind of busy right now...but what the hell, sure, why not, anything for a pal."

She slammed her door, or so she later reported, with a great bang that reverberated through the maidenly structures of the Ellery Street B & B. A guest farther down the hall even stuck out his head, not too happy with the noise.

All the while Dwayne continued with his assignment. In Nadia's ramshackled old house the living room pulsed with children's books and toys, a rocking horse, even a small-scale jungle gym.

Gritting his teeth, he stood facing a smiling Nadia, both hands cupped behind his back grasping Zak's small pistol.

"I sent the baby-sitter home. I'll just check my kiddies, then we can settle down and talk scripts."

"You have *kiddies*?

NADIA
(proudly)
Seven!

DWAYNE
Seven?! Unbelievable!

Nadia laughed. "Well, they're not exactly mine. They're my cousin Lamia's. She's gravely ill, so of course I had to take over. Do you want to see them? We have a little dormitory set up. But first let's stop for a bite. I hope you like borscht and black bread?"

"What could be better?"

"They should all be asleep. The sitter checked before she left. We'll let them settle a bit and then go up there."

Dwayne ate borscht and bread with his new script-writer friend in the dimly lit dining room of the old-fashioned, high-ceiling'd house. The lighting seemed yellowy, as if from a Third-World-level of electricity.

And now he and Nadia stand at the foot of the steep staircase. She whispers "They're so precious in their little beds. Just follow me. Slowly, some of these steps...the children run from two to four, except the new babies, Jorge and Kim."

They mount the steps. He follows, holding the pistol. "I guess you've got some great life insurance, Nadia, what with these kids?"

"This step here sometimes gives an awful groan, could you just...avoid it? We might wake them."

"You have solid insurance? To take care of the babies? In case something..."

They reach the dim upper hallway. Dwayne has the gun pointed directly at her in both shaking hands. She opens the bedroom door, finger to lips. He nearly drops the gun, juggles it desperately, making a saving catch just before it hits the floor. She notices nothing, creeping into the room filled with cradles and basinets. A mother goose night-light on the wall provides an orangey illumination.

From cot to cradle to basinet Dwayne gazes at seven sweetly sleeping, beautiful children, all of different ethnic strains: African, Japanese, Balkan, Indian, Irish....

The handle of the little gun now sticks out of his left trouser pocket.

Nadia, with the lightest touch, kisses each child on the forehead or on the cheek. She looks up at Dwayne with an exalted expression.

Dismissing his cab, Dwayne stumbles into the dimly lit front room at Ellery Street as if he were drunk, shocked to find Zak waiting in an over-stuffed chair in the shadows, his legs stretched out. "Well?" Zak says, "Taken care of? Can we get back to California where it's *warm*? What's it like in here, about thirty degrees?"

"I couldn't do it, Zak. Nobody could. The woman's a saint, she took in seven adopted children from a second cousin who has Bright's Disease — "

"What the fuck is Bright's Disease?"

"Nephritis. Kidneys don't work, you get all puffy and die. Terrible. Let's talk in the morning. I'm ripped. Adriana asleep?"

"Ripped? You're hopeless! This is just the sort of thing that gets me depressed: no follow-through. Damn, you're such a fuckin' softie, Dwayne."

"You'd have felt the same, believe me. Even you. Seven kids she cares for, no time to herself. She gave me borsht..."

"I don't want to hear this shit. *Jesus*, Dwayne!"

"She's got herself a kind of infant U.N. over there."

"I give up, you're hopeless."

"It'll have to be one of the other two...and you'll have to do it, Zak, I know, I know, I'm sorry to be so *hope*less!"

Later the same night, along the sloping second floor of the B & B where the worn carpet seemed the only occupant of the place, Dwayne was stirred awake by a light tapping at his door. He rose, into slippers, robe, groggy he whispered "Who? Who's there?"

He opened the door on its chain to discover Adriana. The girl stood shivering though fully dressed in street clothes. "Couldn't sleep," she told him. "Went for a walk in Harvard Yard." After a hesitation: "I get so tired of this damned virginity, Uncle Vanya."

Meanwhile, back in Arlington, Nadia Senn decides to treat herself to a bubble bath. She's thinking about Dwayne Lipinsky, such a strange, boyish sort of person. So geeky, impossible, really...but somehow — because of the impossibility? — attractive?

She tells herself that she might try to weave a character like him into a script some day.

Returning down the slanty hall from the bathroom, Dwayne finds Adriana already in his bed. Asleep. Her dreadlocks spread out on the pillow. As he goes to pull the covers up over her shoulders he sees that she remained fully dressed, in her street clothes.

She hadn't even removed her shoes.

He gazed down at her for a while...and what? what? He should thrust himself upon her? C'mon.

Delving in her purse he finds the key to her room next door. He turns off the soft glow of the bedside lamp and slowly gets himself out of there.

The next day Adrianna strolled with Dwayne through Harvard Yard after the night of her sleeping in his room at the B&B while he occupied her bed next door. As they looked around at the Harvard buildings they said to each other several times that it wouldn't have been right. "It nearly would have been incest, Uncle," she added. "And please don't tell me The Perfect Guy will shortly come along. I know you'll probably feel obliged to say something like that, but please...just don't?"

They paused reverently before the statue of John Harvard, then sat a while in the Widener Library Reading Room, moved by the atmosphere of holy-hush in that vast, high-ceiling'd place, until she whispered that maybe she should consider going on to college, after all. "'I do love you, Uncle Vanya, I know I had you all *disturbed* last night...my virginity and all that...but it's only been a short while since I thought of you as Mr. Lipinsky of the 11th Grade."

The whole thing left Dwayne feeling morose. Why hadn't she even taken off her shoes?

What happened next was that the three of them traveled by United Airlines to frozen Durango, Colorado in order to make Frankie — the Buddhist scriptwriter — an offer he couldn't refuse.

It turned out that meditative Frankie, once they found him after miles of rented 4-wheel drive, lived in a yurt on a foothill perched above the rustic town of Crestone, famous for its spiritual sites, its stupas, monasteries. Even the town's single fire truck was housed in something called the Kundalini Fire Station.

Frankie. Could he have been simple-minded? Or had he, rather, achieved the condition of a holy man? Yet he did write a movie script, did enter a contest, that much was a worldly-wise activity, wouldn't you say? Dwayne had once tried to read a book that dealt with people like Frankie. It was called *Crazy Wisdom: Spirituality and the Irrational.* Maybe you could call Frankie's way enlightened and at the same time crazy? Is *rational* what blocks the way? In fact, Frankie tended to laugh, they discovered, much in the manner of the Dalai Lama.

CRESTONE, COLORADO – DAY

Frankie is clearly too much of a Salinger-style sweetheart of a genius-kid in his 40's to imagine assaulting in cold blood — even Zak could see such a thing was not humanly possible. On the other hand, how about persuading him to pass in Dwayne's favor? The man planned to donate his movie earnings to a cancer research hospital. He only wrote his script in hopes of being "of benefit." It was entitled THE BUDDHIST GUY and concerned virus-sized "walk-in's" sent to infect certain chosen humans with advanced ideas, like world government, peace, selflessness — to move the planet a little toward sanity, away from galloping consumption-mania and conflict. But there came a glitch: dominated by their chosen carriers, the peace viruses experienced hyper-desirous life in our maniac world and mutated, turning into AGGRESSION-COMPETITION monsters. When the Managers realized that their chosen agents were spreading just the opposite effects from those desired, they tried to get these infected human-carriers to commit suicide...or could there be another solution? An extra-terrestrial operative (BRUCE WILLIS) sets out to hunt them down, take them out before the anti-peace infection spreads....

Zak, Dwayne and Adriana, fascinated, listened to these details of Frankie's project. By the end of the day came a moment steeped in silence while all three of them sat with him on meditation cushions in a state of Samadhi.

Frankie without hesitation offered to withdraw in Dwayne's favor and phoned Spielberg to that effect. After a time the director got back to him. Zak and Adriana and Dwayne listened excitedly but Spielberg wouldn't hear of it. Frankie's was the one winning script that really interested him.

147

SPIELBERG *(on speaker-phone)*
No *chance* of your withdrawing , Frankie. I'll take
you to the mat on that one, your script's got true force,
it shows how people can combine ambition with
soul. I'm thinking of Executive Producing myself.
The contest wants to develop stuff out of the
ordinary and that's what we've got there in your
BUDDHIST GUY. I expect you to be in on
the process every day from start to finish.

FRANKIE *(on phone)*
But listen, Stephen, Dwayne is here visiting
with his friends, and when I think about poor
Dwayne stuck in the role of Standby, what with
his pathetic lifetime failure-history that he's
sketched out, I can't help but have second thoughts.

The three visitors nodded encouragingly, crowding around
Frankie as he made the case for withdrawal.

SPIELBERG *(on phone)*
If it were a matter of that damned shoot-em-
up the others talked me into, sure, I'd let
Roual drop out and we'd pick up on
Dwayne's Standby script, some engaging
ideas in that Custer suicide material of his
— but not yours, Frankie, gosh, we're
definitely planning to see it right through
to Sundance.

"I'm sorry guys," Frankie told them. "Just can't seem to help
out here. But don't rush off. Stay for some brown rice and daikon.
Stephen's so devoted, why, even if I died today he'd still likely

148

make THE BUDDHIST GUY, don't y'think? If I was in, like, an accident? As people are all the time, isn't that right? For nothing's permanent, especially in places like Crestone, Colorado. Even if I were so out of it and not following the whole process as planned, like if I were dead, would that really prevent Stephen from making the film? They'd probably dedicate it to my memory at the end of the credit-crawl."

Here we need to insert a little glimpse of the revolver, its handle now sticking out of Zak's white tube sock.

Adriana stares at Dwayne's clear affection for Frankie as if seeing her former substitute teacher in an entirely new and, he imagined, positive light.

Dwayne himself continued in deep thought, and Frankie, with a sweet smile, gazed meaningfully at the handle of Zak's little gun.

What happened next was that the three of them flew back to California, their final chance being the Frenchman Roual in West Hollywood. But Adrianna, like Frankie, had caught sight of Zak's pistol, which put the situation into a dire perspective for her and she screamed at them in fear and disgust.

"You're both monsters! What were you thinking? I hate you. I'm through with all this stupid stuff."

"Yeah," Dwayne muttered, "it's over, let's just run the rental car into the sea."

Zak was driving on the way out of LAX, Adriana in back with Dwayne. Suddenly she began flailing at Zak with her big fake-Gucci handbag, saving an occasion blow for a slam at Dwayne's head. "Quit it, quit it," the men cried.

"Damn you, Dwayne! You were going to *kill* somebody for the sake of a *movie*! I can't believe it!"

Dwayne grabbed both her hands and held them fast.

149

DWAYNE

Hey — didn't you see how well we treated Frankie?

ADRIANA

So what was the pistol for? Frankie sure understood
he was in danger. You two figure I'm an idiot or
something?

Suddenly Zak pulled the Toyota over into the emergency lane
of the 405. He set the brake, pocketed the key, and walked away
down the freeway without a word, lighting a cigarette.

At which point there arrived an oddity that could only happen in a movie, for aided by mist it seemed to Dwayne that the
Japanese runners from the TV documentary and the JUST F-ING
DO IT book came jogging toward them along the shoulder of the
dark highway.

Zak stood stock still out there as behind him the runners paid
no attention to anyone or anything. Dwayne counted five of the
misty figures continuing at a slow, steady pace, wearing their dia-
per-shorts with daggers tucked in, passing the unobservant Zak,
then the Toyota, then disappearing ahead as heavy traffic on the
405 pounded along toward the Hollywood Freeway.

"Anybody sane would never have considered *murder*," Adriana
told Dwayne as they gazed at Zak out the car window. "And to
bring the girl along as part of a murder plot?! Sure, sure, just lie
to the girl, let her come along to cook and clean and do the laundry... plus pay for the trip!"

"What laundry?"

"That's a manner of speaking, Dwayne. That's a metaphor.
Jeez. Were you really intending to kill that Nadia woman? Insane.
And Frankie? You and Zak are simply insane, Dwayne."

And so the whole project fell apart. No use to mess with Roual,
who from his looks as a self-loving bastard would have been the
best choice for the victim's role in the first place.

Even the death of a winner wouldn't necessarily stop the production of a winning screenplay, Frankie had made the point clear. Later, like many others, Dwayne couldn't resist going to see Raoul's contest-winner, LOTSA GANGBANGERS KILLING PEOPLE. Of the three first-year Spielberg flicks, his turned out to be the only one to trump its weekend and eventually pile up considerable grosses, particularly in Japan.

It wasn't till a year later that Dwayne realized why Adriana had been taking notes so furiously all the while, why she even volunteered to go along on the murder-ride, because the second set of contest-results were being announced on TV just as he thought again about shaking out his squirreled-away pills and preparing hot bath-water for an ultimate giving in to his sense of defeat.

As a kind of final act, there he was watching the second contest finale on the tube, and sure enough, Adriana came on talking about him, ol' Dwayne, her inspiration, without whom, etc. Her submitted script was called...THE STANDBY, screen credit to Adriana Graham. But wait, wait — the TV had started at the bottom of the list, now it was going up to the *actual* three winners: Adriana with her stolen material was to serve as the second year's STANDBY! Once more the Standby? Is there a message here? Dwayne couldn't help it, he felt supremely tickled, perched on the edge of a life-saving fit of laughter. Too much! — now *she'd* have to consider murdering people! As he'd attest, there's nothing like laughter to shake off a destructive final scene.

Dwayne is at the Zen Center up in the Santa Monica mountains now along with seven other aspirants, and for all anyone knows he'll remain right there for the rest of his days. He'd reached the age of thirty-five and was no longer counting. At least he'd had the luck not to kill anybody during the last — he hopes the last — of his Triumph-Hunger-Days.

151

Know what I think? I think it's wonderfully appropriate that Adriana ripped off Dwayne's experience to become the author of what she'd actually titled THE STANDBY, resulting in her actually *becoming* the second year's Standby!

Of course, when Adriana confessed all the details of Zak's hitting on her, that was the end of it for Dwayne and his old cell mate. God knows where Zak is right now. Maybe back at Saldana. But Dwayne finds he can forgive the big man in his heart. In fact, thinking of the whole experience he centers on an imagined glimpse of the holy runners with Zak and Adriana and himself clopping breathily along behind.

    That's a wrap of Dwayne's Movie.

FADE TO WHITE

                                                        THE END

We experience the long credit-crawl petering out with its list of music choices, then the Japanese runners appearing once more with everybody, even the restaurant manager at Dresner's, puffing in line behind them...or wait, for a final image we enter a vast and difficult snowy landscape, black and white out of early Bergman, also influenced by sepia illustrations as if from somebody's grandfather's 1896 edition of *The Inferno*. In this setting we see Dwayne all alone, running his fifty miles up steep, snowy mountain paths, struggling along that hard and demanding way.

Barry Spacks has taught writing and literature for many years at M.I.T. and UCSB. He's published individual poems widely, plus stories, two novels, eleven poetry collections, and three CDs of selected work. His first novel *The Sophomore* has recently been brought back into print in the Faber & Faber *Finds* series.